By

Courtney Lyman

Cover art by Jon Reis Art

But when the fullness of time had come, God sent forth his Son, born of woman, born under the law, to redeem those who were under the law, so that we might receive adoption as sons.

- Galatians 4:4-5

To Lyn Pickering,

My friend and supporter.

More Titles by Courtney Lyman

KW Consulting

Best Laid Plans

Smell the Roses

Dress for Success

Always a Bridesmaid

A Christmas Carol Wedding

Holliday Hotel

Resolution Room

Sweetheart Suite

Resurrection Rest

Book 4 coming May 2019

Christmas Novellas

Christmas Angel

Snowfall

The Twelve Dates of Christmas

CourtneyLyman.com

Dear Reader,

The idea for this story came on me suddenly. Most of my stories are products of my imagination mulling over the idea for months or even years before I sit down and start writing it out. This one sprang to mind so quickly that I knew I had to put aside the story I had planned to write this Christmas and write this instead. There was something about it even from the very beginning that made me eager to share it.

There are little personal touches in this story. Evan being from a small town in Iowa is a reflection of my own story. The first nine years of my life were spent there, and I still love small Midwestern towns – particularly the downtown areas, and the way the communities support one another in ways like coming out for the local high school football games. Speaking of football, that's another element in the story that is a reflection of me. I love many sports including football - especially college football. And Evan's favorite team? Well, that ties back to my roots as well. Although I did have to get in a little cheer for my alma mater while I was at it. You'll have to see if you can spot it.

I had so much fun writing this book. There are so many interesting characters that I loved fleshing out and getting to know. A lot of intelligent, strong women appear in these pages that I could have written much more about. I hope you enjoy reading this book as much as I enjoyed writing it.

After having a few books that dealt with heavier topics like PTSD and death, it was a joy to write something that was lighthearted and fun. I hope this story brightens your Christmas season.

Merry Christmas!

Courtney Lyman

The Ad

"Did you see this?"

Evan Garnett looked up from the history tests he'd been grading to see his sister standing in the doorway of his classroom clutching a newspaper in her hand. As always Kelly was perfectly put together, not a hair out of place, make-up painstakingly natural-looking, and an ensemble that many of his female students would envy.

"I haven't looked at the paper today at all." There was no need to. He knew it had nothing good to say about his football team which hadn't won a game all season. If he didn't love the sport so much, he'd quit coaching. "I assume they're calling for me to be let go."

Kelly looked confused. "What? No, this is more important than football."

Evan somehow doubted that. In a small town like Merryton, Iowa high school football was a big deal. Nearly the whole town turned out for the games, and there hadn't been much to cheer about. "If it's not about football, what is it?"

Kelly smiled triumphantly and laid the paper down on his desk. A full page ad announced applications being taken for some sort of reality show. "Really, Kel? What does this have to do with anything?"

Putting both hands on his desk, Kelly looked at him incredulously. "Did you even read it? It's a dating show, and you need a wife – desperately."

"I'm twenty-eight. I don't think I'm desperate quite yet."

"The fact that you don't realize how desperate you are only intensifies the situation."

"Don't you have clients to work on? Someone needing a dye job or a make-over or something?" Kelly was a wonderful beautician. The girls in his class always wanted her to do their styles for prom and homecoming. Right now he wished she were even busier. Maybe then she'd leave him alone so he could finish grading these tests.

"Nope, I'm free as a bird." She walked over to a desk on the front row and pulled it closer to his desk before sitting down, making herself comfortable and giving every indication of a long chat. Evan sighed. There was nothing to do, but get it over with.

"Okay, fine. You think I need a wife. That still doesn't explain what this has to do with me. All of those dating shows want a pretty boy millionaire as the eligible bachelor. I am certainly not that."

Kelly rolled her eyes. "You didn't even read the ad, did you?" She jabbed her perfectly manicured nail at the newsprint.

We're looking for a man who is upstanding in his community, regardless of income or background to participate in a Christmas time reality show. The man chosen will go on a date with twelve different women resulting in a Christmas Eve special ending in a proposal. This may be your opportunity to find your soul mate.

"Soul mate," he snorted. "Go on one date and find the woman you want to spend the rest of your life with? That's not really an ideal scenario. And you want me to apply for this?"

Kelly nodded vigorously. "And Mom does, too."

Evan groaned. If his mom was on board with this crazy plan, he'd never hear the end of it until he agreed. "Does Dad at least see how ridiculous this is?"

"It doesn't hurt to apply. Maybe they won't even pick you." Her evasion of the question told him that Dad at least agreed with him. "Come on, Evan! You're not going to find anyone in this small town. Make a little effort."

While he still thought this whole scheme was ridiculous, she had a point. Nearly every woman his age in town was married or engaged. His options here were slim. He'd left Merryton to get his teaching degree, and when he came back it seemed like everyone was already coupled up.

He glanced back at the paper. There would be no peace from his mom or his sister if he didn't at least try for it. Chances were there would be somebody more interesting and better suited for this role anyway. The ad said that he needed to create a video application stating his name, age, occupation, hobbies, and hometown. The video should also show him in his day to day life. "Okay, fine. I'll do it. Will you leave now, so I can finish grading and get home?"

Kelly squealed with excitement before coming over to kiss his head. "I thought I'd have to get Mom to help me convince you. Before you do the video, come over to the shop so I can trim your hair. Thank you, Evan! You won't be sorry!" She grabbed the paper and hurried out the door as if afraid he'd change his mind.

He wasn't so sure he should go through with it, but he wouldn't have any peace unless he did. Kelly and his mom were formidable when they ganged up together. His dad was more mild mannered, and even if he was on Evan's side, he would never speak up against the women. No, it was better to do this and let them see for themselves that it was a bad fit.

The Application

"Are you sure you want to do this?" Scott Callahan kept his eyes on the players practicing on the field even as he asked the question.

"Nope, but you know Kelly. I'll never hear the end of it if I don't try." Scott had been Evan's best friend since kindergarten. No one knew the Garnett family better, and there was no one that Evan would trust more with his true feelings.

Scott snorted. "No kidding. Remember that time she was sure you'd look great with highlights? She knows the power of erosion – just keep flowing and eventually you'll wear through rock."

"And we both remember what a disaster that ended up being, too." Evan groaned at the memory. Thankfully he had been able to cut his hair really short to rid himself of his sister's well-intentioned beauty treatment.

"Speaking of Kelly . . ." Scott nudged him in the ribs and nodded to where his sister was marching purposefully across the football field.

"Go tell the team to take a water break, and then start them on a scrimmage while I go talk to Kelly." Scott dutifully started toward the team, blowing his whistle as he went. Evan was grateful to have his best friend be not only his co-worker, but his assistant coach as well.

He always knew the team was in good hands if he ever needed to miss a practice or game. "What are you doing here, Kel?"

She gestured to her phone. "Getting video of you at work."

"Why?"

Kelly rolled her eyes and huffed as if it should be obvious. "For the application video. They want to see the real you, so do whatever it is you do, and forget I'm here."

Evan folded his arms across his chest. "On one condition. Make it easy to forget you're here."

"What do you mean?"

"Don't get up in my face, don't set up a phony, heart-touching scenario, don't mess with my practice."

Placing a hand over her heart, and blinking her hazel eyes, she responded, "Me? Why I would never!"

"Promise."

"I promise, okay?" Kelly smiled. "Just be your normal, charming self, and let me take care of the rest."

Evan wasn't certain that he felt any better about letting her stay, but he figured if she interfered, he'd simply make her leave. As persuasive as she could be, she also knew his limitations and boundaries. He headed back to the field, happy to see that the players were already involved in the scrimmage.

The rest of the practice was spent as normal as possible, and true to her word, Kelly blended into the background so well that Evan was able to forget that she was there as he focused on getting his team ready for the next game.

As the team huddled up at the end of practice, one of the linemen sighed. "I don't know why we're even bothering with all this, Coach. We all know we're going to get beat – again. They're the top team in the division."

Hands on his hips, Evan surveyed the boys in front of him. A few of them nodded in agreement, most of them hung their heads, defeat was already clearly marked on their features. "You are going to get beat." The players looked up in shock. "Already you've made up your minds. You look at the number next to their name, and you've got the ending all planned out. I'm telling you right now that if you come out on Friday night with this attitude you'll lose. You control the outcome." The lineman snorted, and Evan swung his head to look at him. "You got something to say, Jones?"

The boy stood up even as his teammates shook their heads and urged him to let it go. "Coach, we haven't won a game all season. And now you think we can beat the undefeated team in our league? It doesn't make any sense. They're bigger, faster, and flat out better than we are."

"Maybe so. But here's something else, they're cocky. They've already looked past you, and that's when the mighty fall. But if you come out to play with your shoulders drooping, making half-hearted attempts to block or tackle, throwing lazy passes, all because you've already given up, I've got a problem with that. So I'm going to tell you right now, those of you who start, watch your backs. You come out Friday night and play like you expect to lose and I will sit you on the bench so fast your helmet will spin. And those of you who sit the bench, you be ready to play and give me one hundred and ten percent. I'd rather lose knowing we played our hardest and did our best, than win the championship and feel like you didn't play up to your potential." As he spoke, he noticed that several of the boys straightened their shoulders not ready to go down without a fight, and if he only got through to a couple, it was worth it. "Now we're going to play this game as if we expect to win. Bring it in." The players stood and gathered around him. "I know you don't see it, but you've improved throughout this season, and I see potential in you to make a mark. You might be surprised by a win on Friday, but not me. You're ready." The faces staring back at him showed everything from hope to disbelief, pride to discouragement.

The team put their hands in the center of the circle. "LIONS!" the team shouted as one, and for the first time, Evan felt like there was a bit a pride in the chant instead of merely being the mascot of the school. The team headed to the locker room to shower and change. Eyes still on the boys, Evan prayed that he had gotten through to them. Nothing bothered him more than apathy. He could work on their skills, he could draw up plays for their opponents, he could direct which plays they used and when. But if they came out already defeated, there wasn't anything he could do for that.

"Think they believe you?" Scott's eyes were also focused on the team as he stood next to his friend.

"We'll find out on Friday, I guess."

"Do you really think they can beat them?" Scott looked Evan in the eyes.

"I do, but only if they show up to play."

Scott smiled. "Then let's do everything possible to make sure they do."

"That was perfect!" Evan had forgotten that Kelly was even on the field. She had been as good as her word to stay in the background. "You'll be picked for sure."

Evan struggled not to roll his eyes. Leaning his elbow on Evan's shoulder, Scott teased, "How come you didn't ask me to audition for the show, Kelly? I think I'd make a great reality star."

"Oh puh-leeze! Your big head would never fit through the door of the studio – or wherever it is that they'll film. No woman wants an ego like yours in their husband."

"Uh, I beg to differ. Some of the most egotistical men in the world have very beautiful wives – actors, musicians, athletes, politicians."

"Ok, I get your point, but I still don't think you'd be as great on television as Evan."

Scott took a step closer. "Actually I think it's your ego that's fueling this whole thing. If he gets picked you get to say that it was all your doing, and if you can't be on TV yourself, you might as well force a loved one into it so you can live vicariously through them. Don't you agree,

Evan?"

He put his hands up. "I learned a long time ago to stay out of the fights between the two of you."

"You're ridiculous and shallow!" Kelly responded with a flip of her hair as she stomped away.

Scott sighed. "Think she'll ever love me like I love her." It had been a surprise to Evan when he had found out that his best friend had a crush on his sister, and even more shocking when he'd returned from college to find him even more deeply in love with her.

"Not if you keep going on that way," Evan responded.

"What do you mean?" They started walking towards the faculty parking lot.

"Your spars with her are too brotherly. On your end they're flirting, but to her you're just another annoying brother. She's going to need to reevaluate how she sees you." Evan reached his used Honda Civic.

"You're probably right. Time to form a new plan."

"Good luck, Man!" Nothing would please him more than to have his best friend become his brother-in-law, but he knew his sister too well to think that it was going to be easy.

******

Merryton wasn't big enough for a Starbucks, but they had something better. The Ground Floor was a coffee house on the town square with an industrial feel to it that served wonderful black coffee as well as all the froo-froo girly coffee drinks that were so trendy. To top it off, they also had excellent pastries and sandwiches.

Finding a corner with two armchairs and a small table, Evan sat down with his mug of coffee and waited for his dad to arrive. It didn't take long before Nick Garnett was seated next to his son with his own mug of coffee. Nick had thick gray hair, but his other features were so firmly imprinted in his son's face, that Evan had a glimpse into his future every time he saw his dad. Still in uniform as the fire chief for the town, Nick slouched in the chair sighing deeply.

"So what have your mom and/or sister done now?"

"Am I that transparent?"

Nick smiled. "If it weren't one of them, you would've come to the house to talk to me. Having me meet you at The Ground Floor is sort of a give-away."

"Have you heard about this reality program they want me to audition for?" Evan leaned forward, his hand clutched around his mug.

"Once or twice." Nick's lips twitched. "They seem to think you need some help finding a woman."

"What do you think?"

His dad compressed his lips. "I think it's foolish to think you can find the woman that God has for you to be your helpmeet for life on something as superficial as a reality show."

“Thank you!” Evan relaxed back into his seat. He felt vindicated that his dad shared his feelings.

“But I also think that it won’t hurt to audition if for no other reason than it would please the girls. The chances are slim that they’d pick you anyway. No offense meant, but a high school teacher from Iowa isn’t exactly exciting.”

Evan chuckled. “No offense taken. That’s the same conclusion I came to as well.” He sighed and set his empty mug on the table. “What happens if they do pick me?”

“You cross that bridge when you get there. Don’t borrow trouble.” Nick patted his son’s knee. “I’ll be praying that you’ll know what to do if that possibility comes up though.”

“Thanks, Dad.” He shook his head. “I know it’s a long shot, but I keep wondering if I would even accept if they were to choose me.”

“It’d be hard to turn down.” Evan looked at his dad with a wordless question on his face. “I’m guessing they’ll make you a pretty lucrative offer. Plus it’d be pretty flattering to be the one chosen out of hundreds of other men. And it’s an opportunity that doesn’t come up every day.”

“So you think I should do it?”

“I think God will lead you if the time comes. I’m simply warning you that if God says ‘no’, it might not be terribly easy to follow His will when the offer is put out there.” Nick’s eyes twinkled. “Clear as mud?”

"Pretty much." Evan pushed himself to his feet. "Thanks for meeting with me."

"I wondered when you'd finally talk to me about this deal." Nick shook his head. "I'd never have guessed this would be something we'd be discussing."

Evan walked outside to the brisk fall air. The decision would have to be made soon. To be a Christmas special everything would have to come together quickly. He only hoped he would have complete clarity if he was offered the chance. Laughing at himself, he was reminded that the chances of him being chosen were extremely remote anyway. His dad was right. He was borrowing trouble.

******

Kelly followed him around the rest of the week. She interviewed him, taped his history classes, showed him in church, and culminated in the big football game on Friday. To her credit, other than the interview, Evan was nearly unaware of her presence. He had half expected her to be a superstar director of her film and try to make him something he wasn't. Apparently, she really felt like he was perfect for the show the way he was.

The game on Friday was packed. Even though the team hadn't been performing well, the town still came out in support, and Evan was only aware of a few grumblers that complained about the team's record. The cheerleaders were as perky as if they were undefeated. He found himself wondering if the cheerleaders were even aware of the game or if it was an opportunity for them to perform. Maybe they did both.

He had been pleased with the team in the locker room. They were pumped up for the game, excited to prove their coach right, with only a small amount of nerves visible. Only one player didn't seem to share his teammates' enthusiasm. Javon Jones, the lineman who had raised questions at the practice, was obviously lacking any excitement or motivation. Showing up late, and going through warm ups with a lackluster effort, Evan knew he had to make a difficult, and most likely unpopular decision.

"Javon, come here!" The player jogged over to the bench. Truth be told, Javon was possibly the most talented player on the team, and definitely the largest. Most of the town would think that sitting him would be giving up, but Javon had already given up, and he couldn't have him infecting the rest of the team. "I want you to sit."

"Sit? For how long?"

"I haven't decided yet. It kind of depends on your attitude. You've got defeat written all over you. I can't play you like that. That was something we already discussed in practice. You don't show effort, you don't play."

Javon smirked. "Have you seen those guys? They're twice the size of anyone of our guys. You sit me, and you're sure to lose."

"According to you, we'll lose either way, so I'll take my chances with someone who is willing to give it his all. Sit." Before the boy could respond, Evan walked away. Grabbing the jersey of another player, he pulled him closer. Tyrone Little wasn't as athletic or as big as Javon, but the boy put his heart and soul into each practice. When he was on the bench, he was cheering harder than any cheerleader, and always had an encouraging word for each of his teammates. And he was willing to do anything his coaches asked of him. "You're starting, Tyrone."

Tyrone's eyes grew big. "Are you serious, Coach?"

"Absolutely. You've earned it."

He let out a cheer that drew the attention of the first ten rows of the bleachers. "Thank you, Coach, thank you!"

As he rushed out onto the field, Scott stepped up next to Evan. "Are you certain about this? You tell the boys we can win, then sit our best player. Seems like it's counterproductive."

"Did you see Javon in warm ups? He wasn't even trying. That laziness, and apathy can spread quicker than the flu. I'm not going to allow him to infect the rest of the boys. Especially since they finally believe they might have a chance."

Scott nodded, and moved on. Saying a quick prayer, Evan hoped he hadn't made a decision that would cost him his job.

As the first play was snapped, Tyrone surged forward taking down the runner before he could cross the line of scrimmage. On the second play, Tyrone pushed through the offensive line and put pressure on the quarterback causing him to throw the ball away. By the third down, the crowd was on its feet, cheering on this benchwarmer who was playing tougher than anyone had expected. Third down resulted in a stopped run play, and the number one team in the league was forced to punt after a quick three and out.

The Merryton crowd was ecstatically cheering. The defense had rarely made a stop in previous games. This was a victory in itself. Scott thumped Evan on the back. “Good decision. Tyrone is eager to prove he’s capable.”

Evan shook his head. “No, Tyrone wants his team to rise to the occasion. It’s not about him.” He nodded to the sideline where the team was surrounding Tyrone. The young man was encouraging them, urging the offense to take advantage of the stop, and pumping them up. Further down on the bench, Javon sulked. Evan breathed deeply. “Let’s do this!”

By halftime, Merryton was elated. Their high school was leading the top team twenty-one to seven. As Evan watched the other team head to the locker room, he noticed the slumped shoulders of defeat, heads shaking in disbelief, anger, and frustration. The coaches’ faces revealed frustration and confusion.

In their own locker room, the boys were celebrating. Evan raised his hands and the team quieted down. “I’m so proud of you guys! I knew this was in you, and what a great time for it to emerge. But we still have another half to play. Don’t stop! Keep up this effort. Those guys don’t know what hit them, but I can guarantee they’re going to come out fired up and ready to take this game back. But this is our game, and they can’t have it!” The boys cheered wildly. “Let’s go back out there and show them just how tough the Merryton Mountain Lions can be!”

As he watched the confidence and enthusiasm in the team as they surged back out towards the field, he felt assured that they would at least play as hard as they could even if they didn't pull off the win. What a fantastic time for the team to seize their potential!

"Coach?" The quiet voice caught Evan's attention. He turned to see Javon standing with his helmet in hand. "I'm ready to give it my best shot – if you want to play me."

Evan was torn. He was happy to see the attitude change in Javon, and he was a good player, but Tyrone had done such a good job. He didn't want to sit him after all the work he'd done in the first half. A hand on his shoulder startled him. Tyrone smiled at him. "It's okay, Coach. Javon needs this chance." It was as if the young man had heard Evan's inner dialogue.

Suddenly, Evan realized it was true. Javon was a senior. A good showing at this game could be enough to make a difference in whether he earned a scholarship or not. Tyrone had done his job. "Okay, Jones. You're in."

Javon smiled broadly. "I won't let you down." He hurried off to join the team.

"I need you to keep pumping the team up, Tyrone. They're responding to you. You'll make a good coach someday."

Tyrone brushed off the compliment. "Nah, Coach. They're responding to you. You told us we could do it, and we believed you." With that, the young man took his place with the team.

True to his word, Javon showed up in a way he never had before. If they had been impressed with Tyrone's defense, they were stunned by Javon. The boy played with an intensity that had been lacking in previous games. He seemed to know exactly where he should be to make the best play possible. Evan couldn't be prouder of this team.

When the final whistle was blown, the score was astonishing – forty-two to fourteen. The number one team had fallen, heading back to the bus with drooping shoulders. Merryton was celebrating ecstatically. The students rushed onto the field to congratulate their schoolmates. The adults talked over the game focusing on the tremendous defense shown by first Tyrone and then Javon, and wondering at the crazy strategy of the coach that had somehow worked.

"That was exactly what your audition tape needed," Kelly spoke up from behind him. He turned from the excitement on the field to his sister's beaming face. "A David and Goliath story, a coach who got the very best out of his team when it mattered most – it's gold!"

"Well, I'm glad you're pleased." He turned back to face his team. "Look at them! They're standing tall for the first time this season, and nothing can take this victory away from them. This will be a game they tell their grandchildren about. That's what matters to me."

"Yes! I swear you're perfect for reality television. They won't need to script hardly any of your lines. You instinctively know what to say." Evan hadn't even noticed that his sister still had her phone out and had recorded what he had said. "That's why *some* people shouldn't be on TV." At her pointed statement, Evan was aware that Scott was behind him.

"You're right. Evan has a way of saying the right thing at the right time. It's a skill many lack – including myself."

Kelly's mouth dropped open. "Are you feeling okay?"

Scott smiled. "Maybe I'm growing up." He turned back to Evan. "The boys are going to The Barn to celebrate. Wanna come?"

"Absolutely!" The Barn was actually an old barn that had been torn down and rebuilt at the edge of town. They served pizza and burgers as well as a wide array of ice cream flavors. It was a favorite hangout for the students.

By the time he got there, The Barn was filled nearly to capacity. He squeezed through the crowd being congratulated on every side as he pushed through to get to the team. Several pizzas were delivered to the tables set up for the team by the owner. "It's on the house, boys! Great game!" The boys cheered and thanked the owner who took a picture of the team to hang up on the walls. "We'll remember this game for a long time." As he passed Evan, he thumped his shoulder. "Great coaching! I wasn't sure when you sat Jones, but it turned out to be exactly what this team needed."

Evan shook his head. "They needed to believe they could do it. This will be a turning point unless I miss my guess." He went around the tables congratulating, praising, and teasing his boys personally before he got the attention of the whole team. Without Evan being aware of it, the whole restaurant quieted down to pay attention to the coach. "Boys, the giant has fallen and the Mountain Lions are victorious!" They cheered loudly, pounding on the table. "Today was a great game to watch, not only because it was our first win of the season, or because we took down number one," he paused as the team cheered again, "but because I saw you stand up and do what I knew you were capable of doing. There's no going back now! We've all seen what you can do. This is the new beginning of our season. And we're not who we were! We are strong. We are capable. We are Lions!" The entire restaurant erupted in cheers.

Scott shook his head. "She's right. You know what to say." He nodded to where Kelly was recording the celebration. "I don't know, Man. You might need to think about if you're going to accept this gig or not if it's offered to you. You're very personable. They might actually choose you."

Evan sighed. "I highly doubt that's a possibility."

The Director

The video showed what seemed like the whole town celebrating the football team's win. Eliana Santos tilted her head critically as she watched. The coach was attractive with his light brown hair that probably had natural blonde highlights in the summer and brown eyes. He was fit and had a brilliant smile that lit his eyes. Watching him interact with his players he seemed to genuinely care about each of them. The town obviously adored him.

She sighed. "I hadn't considered having a teacher, but this guy is a good candidate."

Penelope Rivera watched the screen dreamily. "He really is." Eliana shook her head. Penny was her assistant director, but she might have to watch that *she* didn't fall in love with whoever was picked to be their bachelor.

"It'd be different. He certainly isn't a millionaire or likely to be one if he continues teaching high school in a small town. It might be the difference we need." It had amazed Eliana that so many men had applied. Too often they turned off the tape five minutes in as the man came across arrogant or rude or ignorant. She tried not to let looks persuade her, but in all honesty it was television, and ratings were better when pretty people were on the screen. There had been several videos that had caught their attention, but there was something special about this one. "What is it about this guy that makes him stand out?" she wondered aloud.

"He's real." Penny looked at her. "Nothing seems forced or scripted. Everything on here has been as if he wasn't even aware the camera was on him, and yet he was perfect."

She was right. He did everything as if he wasn't even aware that he was being filmed which was a huge advantage for her show. "Put him on the list." Penny wrote something down and they moved on.

This part was tedious, but Eliana wanted to be part of it. She was afraid that someone else might not see the potential of someone because they weren't Hollywood beautiful or toss them aside because of their occupation – someone like Evan Garnett might be turned down. There was so much more that she was looking for than looks and wealth. She wanted this show to stand out by having a normal guy who the nation could fall in love with. Because of her determination, she wanted to be involved with the selection of just who that would be.

It was past midnight when Eliana rubbed a hand across her tired eyes and yawned. "How many have we narrowed it down to?"

Penny looked at her list. "We have ten."

"That's a nice round number. Tomorrow let's schedule a trip to visit each one in person. I don't want them to know we're coming so that they'll be as natural as possible. Hopefully by the end we'll know exactly which guy we want." Eliana patted Penny on the shoulder. "Thanks for staying late so we could get this done."

"Who knew it'd be exhausting sorting through a bunch of gorgeous guys?"

Eliana smiled. Penny sometimes made her think of boy crazy high school girl. "We're not looking for just any guy. We're looking for the perfect guy which is why it's so exhausting. They have to be more than a pretty face." She stood up and stretched. "Don't fall in love with them!" she warned. "They're supposed to pick another girl by the end of the show."

"I know. A Christmas proposal," she sighed. "It's so romantic."

Eliana wasn't sure how romantic it was. All she knew was it was her job for now, and if she did it well, she might get a shot at something bigger. It was a means to an end. She did not want to be directing reality TV the rest of her career.

The next day, Eliana and Penny made arrangements to travel to ten locations. Anyone could put together a good audition tape – well maybe not 'anyone', there had been a lot of bad ones – but on tape things could be edited and hidden that couldn't be in person. Especially since their visit was unexpected.

While they made the plans, Eliana looked over the list. There was a cowboy from Texas who was on the professional rodeo circuit, a politician from Alabama, a minor league baseball player from Florida, an up-and-coming country singer from Tennessee, a lawyer from Maryland, a racecar driver from Ohio, a doctor from Montana, a business owner from Washington, a firefighter from Colorado, and then the teacher/coach from Iowa. Looking over the list the teacher certainly appeared to be the least interesting, but there was something that kept drawing her back to him. His name consistently jumped out to her as if lit up on the page. "Let's go to Iowa last. I know it's not ideal, but I have a good feeling about him."

Penny squealed. "He was one of my favorites, too." She looked over the list. "And the firefighter. Ooh, and the cowboy. Oh, and the singer."

Eliana held up her hand. "Okay, Penny. I think you'll enjoy this trip more than I will." Penny simply grinned and tossed her dark shoulder-length hair before returning to the computer to get their tickets set.

This job had come up suddenly. The original director had backed out for unknown reasons although rumor had it that she had demanded more money than the studio was willing to give to this product. The producer had then requested her. Eliana had been flattered and eager to try her hand at reality television. She had a definite vision of what she wanted this to look like, and thankfully the producer had agreed with it. She knew she was chosen partially because she was a female which would be the target audience. But romance left her cold. She only hoped that this would lead to something bigger and eventually she could direct something truly epic, something memorable, something worthwhile.

Unlike Penny, she did not look forward to meeting

these final ten men. She had a feeling that some of them would be an absolute disappointment once she saw them in person. Her hope was that one of them would be at least worth pursuing. If not, she'd have to pick the best and make him into a hero the best she knew how. She wanted to it to be as unscripted as possible, but if she had to settle for good enough, she may have to rely on scripts to make him look better.

******

The two women started their trip in Washington where they visited a shop called Ray's Ways. The shop sold eclectic merchandise from all over the world – everything from an English tea set to African instruments to Indian saris could be found in his shop. It had proved to be so popular in Seattle that he had opened two more locations.

Ray Browning had claimed in his video that he traveled to these far off places and purchased only what was made in ethical ways. No child labor or sweatshop produced items were allowed in his stores.

As they entered, signs proclaimed this fact to everyone, and looking at the price tags Eliana wondered if the signs were there to give credence to the outrageously high prices. After browsing for a while, Eliana approached a young woman who worked at the store.

"I heard about this store recently. I was wondering if it's true that Ray Browning does the traveling to these locations to purchase the inventory?"

The woman, whose name tag said she was Sophie,

snorted. “I don’t think he’s ever left the state of Washington.”

“Really? Why would he claim he had?” This was exactly what Eliana had feared. The men on the videos were all too good to be true.

“He says it’s a chick magnet if they think he’s been to exotic locations.” She rolled her eyes.

“Wow. That’s good to know. Do you like working for him?”

She shrugged. “He pays okay, and there’s always new stuff coming in so I guess it’s not terrible. It’ll get me through college anyway.”

“What’s he like?”

“Ray? Boring.” Sophie looked around and leaned forward to whisper, “We went on a date once, but all he could talk about was himself. I think he’s dated every girl he hires – which is most of the staff.”

“Interesting.”

As if suddenly realizing that she was gossiping with a complete stranger, Sophie straightened. “Can I help you with anything?”

“You already have. Thank you so much.”

Sophie looked worried. “I hope I didn’t get him into trouble.”

“No, nothing like that.” She leaned forward, and said

confidentially, "It's a dating thing."

"Oh, yeah, you do not want to go down that road. Meet online?"

"Something like that." Eliana grabbed Penny. In the car, she told Penny what Sophie had said about Ray.

"Do you believe her?" Penny asked. "Maybe it's sour grapes, you know?"

"That's why we're going to his other store, and I'm hoping to meet him in person, too. But it's not looking great for him."

The employees at the other store had a similar opinion of Ray to Sophie's. To the best of their knowledge, Ray had never left the state let alone the country, and many of the girls had dated him only once after finding that he had a narcissistic personality that was a real turn off. There was a business office, and Eliana had been assured that she could find Ray there if she wanted to meet him in person.

"This guy doesn't sound a lot like his video, does he?" Penny reluctantly admitted. "How disappointing."

Eliana sighed. "I have a bad feeling that most of these men are going to be disappointment."

Ray's personal secretary was beautiful if a bit overdone. Her makeup was too perfect, hair a brilliant shade of blonde that must cost a fortune at the salon, her clothes a bit too tight, her heels absurdly high, and if all of that wasn't enough, she spoke in a whispery voice as if imitating

Marilyn Monroe. While they waited to see Ray Browning all his secretary did was play on her phone making Eliana wonder if the woman's position was necessary or simply window-dressing.

When the phone buzzed, Miss Marilyn-Monroe-wannabe waved them back lazily. Ray stood tall by his desk, straightening even more when he saw the two women enter his office. A smile that made Eliana's skin crawl lit his face. "Well, this is a pleasure to have two lovely ladies in my office. What can I do for you?" Even Penny frowned slightly at the insincere compliment.

"I saw something on you recently and had some questions for you," Eliana began with a smile.

"Oh, a reporter?" He puffed out his chest comically.

"I'm with the media in a fashion." Eliana didn't really want to lie, but she didn't want him knowing that she was with *The Twelve Dates of Christmas*. He'd only put on his best behavior, and she'd be no closer to the truth than before. "You've said that you've traveled the world. Which was your favorite location to visit?"

Ray leaned back in his chair. "Wow. That's difficult." His eyes glanced around the room at the posters of exotic locations. Gesturing at one, he said, "I'd have to say Egypt. There's a certain thrill that comes with searching through the streets of Cairo. I feel like an archeologist, or a treasure hunter." He looked at their faces as if weighing their reactions.

"That does sound exciting. Which of the archeological

sites did you find the most fascinating?"

His eyes narrowed briefly. "There are so many it's hard to choose, isn't it?"

"I personally liked visiting Agilkia Island. I find it fascinating that they moved the whole site due to flooding, don't you?"

"I stick pretty close to Cairo. Big city, lots of opportunity," he evaded.

"Of course. Cairo – the City of the Thousand . . ." she left the saying hanging for him to finish.

Ray stood abruptly. "As much fun as this is, I really haven't got time to reminisce."

Eliana stood as well. "That's a shame. I'd love to see your pictures some time. You must have some interesting stories to share." As he led them to the doors, she tried one more thing. "Women must find your travel stories intriguing."

His smile was forced and a bead of sweat trickled down his head. "They do, and I would love to share them with you, but like I said, I'm a busy man."

"Of course. Maybe some other time." As Eliana passed the secretary, she approached her. "Where is your world traveling boss off to next?"

An unladylike snort erupted from the pristine assistant. "I don't know. Puget Sound?" She glanced up from her phone for a brief moment. "It would make my job more interesting if he *would* actually leave from time to time."

Eliana felt secure in her decision that this was not the right guy for her show. She only hoped that they weren't all like this.

Unfortunately, her hopes were dashed one by one. The doctor was under investigation. The firefighter was brash, arrogant, and crude. The rodeo cowboy was a has-been who was in denial. She had never had much hope for the politician or the lawyer, and they both lived up to their stereotypes. The singer was a waiter like many up and coming superstars, but unlike them, a trip to hear him sing in a bar revealed that he had no talent to help him on his way. A recent crash had left the racecar driver in the hospital, and it was unlikely he would be well enough by the time they needed to start filming. Only the baseball player had been somewhat intriguing until they found several women who all claimed to be his girlfriend already.

Penny sat back in her seat on the airplane, the very picture of dejection. "I would have never guessed it would be this hard."

"Well, we have one more guy to check out." Eliana reviewed the application for Evan Garnett. She didn't know why, but she had high hopes that this was the right guy. There had been a feeling in his video of reluctance that she found refreshing. He hadn't talked about himself, instead others had spoken of him in glowing terms with a sincerity that was unmistakable.

"But what if he's a fake, too." Penny's wail penetrated

Eliana's thoughts.

"Then we talk it over. Maybe the cowboy could be made to work. Or the baseball player. Surely all his girlfriends would drop him once he's on the show."

"Yeah, and he'll make tabloids afterwards by being caught with all the other girls after he proposes." Penny shook her head in disgust.

"That's not really our fault. These TV hook-ups rarely actually make it to the wedding before they break-up." Eliana didn't take her eyes off the picture of Evan. "But I can't see this guy not working out."

"How is he any different?" Penny leaned over to look at the picture.

"I'm not sure. I keep going back to his video and thinking that he was the only one who didn't brag on himself. It was the rest of the town that seemed to have things to say about him." The truth was that she was drawn to him in a way that she hadn't been drawn to anyone else. He was attractive, kind, humble, and smart. What girl wouldn't be interested in someone like him?

The Surprise Visit

There are two women asking about you around town.

Evan glanced at his phone. This was the fifth text he'd received about these women. What was going on? It hit him that this could possibly be related to the reality show Kelly entered him in, but he hadn't heard anything from the show. He sighed as he put the papers he needed to grade in his bag.

He swung the door to his classroom open and heard an expression of pain as the door came in contact with someone coming up the hall. Horrified, he closed the door to see who had been injured by his carelessness. A woman with black hair tied back in a long braid down her back clutched both hands over her face. Another younger woman stood next to her with her hand covering her mouth whether it was to hide her laughter or in concern was unclear.

"I am so sorry!" He took the woman by the elbow and led her to a desk and sat her down. "Are you bleeding or need ice or . . ." Feeling helpless he glanced over at the other woman who was now obviously trying to hide her laughter.

The woman felt her nose tentatively. "I don't think it's bleeding. Does it look bad?"

Evan leaned forward. Her nose was definitely red, but

not swollen. Breathing a sigh of relief, he said, "I think it's okay."

The other woman stepped forward and took a look. "I don't think it's broken or anything."

The injured woman sighed, brought her hand up as if to touch it again, then put her hand back down. It suddenly occurred to Evan that these two women may well be the very ones who had been asking about him all day. Pulling himself up to his full height and withdrawing suspiciously, he asked, "Can I help you with anything?"

The younger girl giggled, but was silenced with a glare from the older one. "Could you please sit down so we could talk?"

Evan reluctantly sat at his desk at the front of the room wanting some distance between himself and these two women. They seemed harmless enough, but you never could tell these days.

The woman who seemed to be in charge rubbed her nose one more time before fixing her gaze on him. Even with her nose a light shade of pink from her encounter with his door, she was a beautiful woman. Her eyes were almond shaped and such a deep brown they were nearly black fringed with thick black lashes. Her lips were full and her skin was tan. He had a hard time believing that she was here to cause problems.

"You're very well-protected in this town," she began with a smile. Maybe he was wrong. Perhaps she was intending to cause trouble. "I'm going to have to do something I haven't done with this project and lay my cards on the table to get any information."

Evan's eyes narrowed. "I'd certainly like for you to tell me what's going on." He folded her arms across his chest.

"I'm Eliana Santos, the director of *The Twelve Dates of Christmas*." Surprise took Evan's voice as he leaned back in his desk chair. He had briefly wondered if these two women had anything to do with the reality show, but quickly dismissed it. It seems like he should learn to listen to his gut more often. "This is Penelope Rivera, my assistant."

"Call me Penny," the younger girl stated, looking at him with open admiration.

"All of the other candidates we could get other people to talk about before we met with them personally. Even when we met with them we were able to conceal our identity so we could get a better idea of who they were without them trying to impress us." Eliana smiled and leaned forward in the desk, clasping her hands together. "But you, no one would give us any information about. I began to be scared that they would find a reason to have us arrested."

Evan smiled. "I've received multiple texts about you two," he confirmed. "Merryton's pretty small. Strangers stand out."

One of Eliana's eyebrows raised. "I noticed that, which is why I decided to be perfectly honest with you. If I tried to be subtle with you, I was afraid you'd run me out of town." She chuckled, and he smiled sympathetically.

"What sorts of things did you want to know? You already know all about me from my application."

Eliana stood and came close to his desk. "I know about you – where you work, where you live, your hobbies – but I don't know *you*. Too often guys will send in their applications and they seem perfect, but when we meet them in person we find that their persona they represented to us and who they truly are look very different."

Drumming his fingers on the desk, Evan watched Eliana. Penny was nodding in agreement, disappointment turning her mouth down. "It's television. Personas are more important than reality. Everyone knows that even reality TV is more scripted than it's supposed to appear," Evan pointed out.

Eliana shook her head. "Maybe for most shows, but not mine. I don't want a persona, I want a true person who is as desirable off screen as he is on. I want the scripting to be absolutely minimal. I want to show women that there are normal men in the world who are even more attractive than the superstars or billionaires or athletes because they're real, and sweet, and kind." Her voice softened by the end and her eyes locked in on his. They seemed to be urging him to be that guy, to show her that her dream existed. His heart rate sped up. Was he that guy? Could he be that guy?

"I'm still not sure I'm the one you want. I'm nothing more than a teacher who coaches a football team in a small town in the Midwest. There has to be someone who is more desirable than me."

Penny snorted. "There's not!"

"We'd like to simply spend time with you today. Maybe by the end we'll agree with you, and we'll move on, but if not, I'd like you to at least consider the possibility. I mean, why enter your information if you didn't want to be a part of this?"

Evan sighed. "I think you need to meet my sister."

******

Kelly squealed loudly causing Eliana and Penny to flinch. "I knew he'd be perfect. I told you you'd be perfect." She danced around the room and Evan was thankful he had found her at home and not at the salon.

"This doesn't necessarily mean anything. Don't make too much of it."

Kelly stopped and stared at him as if he just uttered the most nonsensical sentence she had ever heard. "What do you mean?"

"They've been visiting all the applicants."

"Just ten," Penny clarified. "We narrowed it down to ten."

Kelly's face lit up. "You're in the top ten!"

Evan stifled a groan. "That means there are nine other guys that have just as much chance of getting picked."

"Not really," Penny muttered before Eliana smacked her arm.

But Kelly had heard it. "What do you mean 'not really'? Are there less than nine? Is he the 'one'?"

Eliana sighed and glared at Penny before answering Kelly's questions. "We have visited the ten most promising candidates, and to be truthful most of them were . . ." she paused as if trying to find the right word. "Uninspiring." Penny shuddered making Evan wonder just how bad the other candidates were. "However, that doesn't mean that your brother is automatically 'the one'." She drew air quotes around the words. "We need to get to know him better. We may decide that he's not what we're looking for either. Besides that, even if we choose him, he is under no obligation to be part of it."

Kelly whipped her head back to her brother. Slowly approaching him, she pulled herself up to her full height sticking her finger in his chest. "You'd better do it if they offer it to you."

Evan's mouth tipped on one side as he looked down at his sister. "At the risk of appearing juvenile, you're not the boss of me. I can do whatever I want." He saw Eliana's amusement at his response. Honestly, he didn't know if he wanted her to be impressed with what she saw or disappointed in him. On the one hand, he wasn't even sure he wanted to do the show. But on the other hand, he didn't want Eliana thinking badly of him, although he wasn't sure why that was important.

Kelly shrugged. "That's okay. I've got mom on my

side." Seeming to think that she had won that argument, she turned her attention back to the women before he could reply. "So what happens now?"

"We don't really want the town knowing why we're here. We'd like to hear from them about Evan without the desire to build him up too much. And we need to see Evan in action." When Eliana explained it that way it didn't seem too difficult, but Evan saw the gleam in Kelly's eyes.

"Kelly, you won't tell anyone who Eliana and Penny really are, right?" Evan warned.

"I hope not," Eliana jumped in before Kelly could respond. "It would be a shame to have to eliminate you because your family couldn't follow the rules."

Evan wasn't sure if it was an actual rule or a preference, but he was certain now that neither Kelly nor his mother would give it away. He smiled at Eliana's warning, and it only broadened when Kelly hurriedly assured them that she would never tell.

"I need to go get ready for the football game tonight," Evan said, "but I'm sure I'll see you ladies around." He ducked out leaving Kelly in charge of their guests. With Eliana's warning going through her mind, he was certain they were in the best hands.

The Town

Eliana followed Kelly into The Ground Floor, the local coffee shop, and inhaled deeply. She loved the smell of coffee, and the feel of coffee houses. Local ones were the best she had discovered in her travels. She loved their atmosphere and their attention to detail. Plus their coffee tended to be better, deeper, richer, and more complex than chain coffee houses.

She didn't tell Kelly that they had already visited the coffee shop, hoping someone would talk to them about Evan, but had been shut down quickly. The same barista who had spoken to them earlier was still behind the counter. The lanky college-aged boy eyed them suspiciously when he saw that they were with Evan's sister, but he welcomed them in a pleasant fashion.

"I see you found Coach Garnett's sister," he remarked.

"Oh, have you guys already met?" Kelly seemed disappointed.

"Sort of," Eliana replied. "I think we made poor," she glanced at his nametag, "Braden uncomfortable when we started asking about Evan. I can tell he's very loyal to the Garnett family."

Kelly beamed. "I suppose it does seem weird to have people asking about us, but it's okay, Braden. This is Eliana and Penny. They're some friends visiting us."

Braden's eyes narrowed. "How'd you meet?"

"Online," Eliana answered without hesitation. "They're interested in a project I'm working on. We've hit it off rather quickly."

Suspicion lifted from Braden's face. "They're easy people to like, and if they're interested in your project it must be good. Coach Garnett is a good judge of character."

"Braden was Evan's star quarterback two years ago," Kelly bragged on the boy.

He flushed at her praise. "I wasn't a star, but Coach can make any of us play better. If it wasn't for him, I might still be in high school." He chuckled slightly. "I was failing just about everything, but gym. He got me tutors, and helped me raise my grades. He says it was so that I wouldn't be academically ineligible, but I think he really was concerned about my future. When I took my diploma, he was the one cheering the loudest." Shaking himself, he remembered his job. "Can I get you ladies anything?"

After placing their orders, the women found a table and sat down. "I hope you don't mind, but I invited my dad over. He's the fire chief so he works across the town square from here. I want you to meet him." Kelly looked at Eliana intently. "But I swear I didn't tell him anything about your project."

Eliana smiled. Her warning was certainly doing the trick as far as Kelly was concerned. "I'd love to meet your father. And our agreement doesn't extend to family. Your parents can know about it."

Kelly breathed a sigh of relief. "Thank goodness! I wasn't sure how I was going to keep it a secret from everyone! Having Mom and Dad to talk to will be so helpful!"

"Just remind them about the rule so they don't ruin Evan's chances on accident."

Kelly's eyes widened. "Oh, of course." Eliana was pleased that she had thought up that rule to help prevent their purpose for being there spreading throughout the entire town or to the other candidates.

A man walked in that reminded Eliana so much of Evan that she was certain it was his father. If she had any doubt, his uniform would have clinched it. He nodded over to Braden who immediately began making a mug of black coffee for the fire chief.

With the mug of coffee in hand, Evan's dad made his way over to sit with the women. He kissed his daughter on the cheek, then shook hands with the other two. "So what's going on?"

"I wanted you to meet Eliana Santos and Penny Rivera. This is my dad, Nicolas Garnett," Kelly said, enthusiasm lacing every word. Lowering her voice, she continued. "They're with the show."

Evan's dad raised his eyebrows. "What exactly does that mean?"

"He's a finalist, but it's a big secret. We can't tell anyone or it will ruin his chances." Kelly kept her voice soft, nearly to a whisper.

"I see. So what part do you two play?" Nicolas wrapped his hands around his mug and Eliana felt like she was the one being interviewed, which she supposed she was. A dad would want more information before sending his son off on something like this.

Leaning forward, Eliana tried to relieve any of his fears. Evan was by far the best candidate they had. She didn't want to lose him, because his father had concerns. "I'm the director, and Penny is my assistant." Penny smiled and waved. "I appreciate you meeting with us."

Nicolas nodded. "What do you expect to get out of this program?"

Eliana raised her eyebrows. He was certainly direct. She could be direct as well. "Personally, professionally, or for Evan?"

Nicolas tried to hide his smile. He apparently appreciated her willingness to be forthright with him. "How about all three?"

"Personally, I hope to create a program that is enjoyable to watch during the Christmas season, something that families can sit down and watch together. Professionally, I hope that it will lead to better directing jobs, and not more reality shows. For Evan . . ." She paused and thought for a moment. What did she want for him? "I want him to have an enjoyable experience, and possibly find someone that he can love."

"What happens if he can't find a woman he can love?"

Eliana picked up her mug of coffee and took a sip,

stalling for time. “I’ll do my best to find women he can respect. Unfortunately the show has to end in a proposal. It’s what everyone is waiting for and anticipating, but a proposal can be retracted if he isn’t completely sure.”

Nicolas set his mug down. “Has Evan explained to you our beliefs?” At Eliana’s negative, he continued. “We’re Christians. We expect purity, and it’s going to be important that any woman he marries shares our faith.”

Smiling, Eliana met his eyes. “I share your beliefs as well, and I’m going to do everything I can to find women who would feel the same way. I also have a plan to make it almost impossible for these women to try to anything that would make Evan uncomfortable or put him in an awkward situation.”

For the first time, Nicolas smiled. “That’s good to hear.” He glanced down at her mug, then looked back up in surprise. “Black coffee?”

Eliana smiled slightly. “Only when it’s good.”

Throwing his back, he laughed heartily. “Make sure you pick up a bag of beans before you head home.” He drained the last of his mug before standing. “I need to get back to work, Kel-Bel.” He patted her on the shoulder and waved good-bye to the women. Eliana felt confident that Evan wouldn’t get discouragement from his dad at least.

Being with Kelly proved to be an advantage for the two women in Merryton. People were pleased to meet them, their suspicions allayed by the presence of a member of the Garnett family which appeared to be highly respected in the small community. Not only did they speak highly of Evan, but of the whole family.

"Did you know that there have been five members of the Garnett family who have served in politics in this state?" one man told them proudly. Kelly had introduced him as the current mayor, but for the life of Eliana she couldn't remember his name. "Fortunately for me, none of this generation seem to be interested in politics," he teased nudging Kelly's arm.

Kelly smiled tightly. "Not yet anyway." The mayor's face dropped for a minute before he passed it off as a joke and continued on with the conversation which he managed to make about his own political accomplishments rather than about Evan.

As Kelly pulled the two women away, she murmured, "Evan would beat him hands down if he ever chose to run."

"Does he have political ambitions?" Eliana asked.

"No," Kelly sighed, "but he'd be good at it if he did."

Not a person in town had a bad thing to say about Evan. Eliana began to wonder if Kelly had broken their deal and told everyone who they were. As they entered the bleachers for the football game Eliana heard two older women talking in front of them.

"Do you think Coach has a shot at that reality show his sister signed him up for?"

The other shook her head reluctantly. "Nah, they

look for guys with more drama than Evan. They want a womanizer who'll make out with every woman they throw his way. He's not that type."

The first lady sighed. "It would be nice if they would pick him though. He's not only cute, he's a gentleman. They seem to be in short supply these days. Did I tell you that the other day he helped me load my groceries in my car. If he was only forty years older," she sighed with a giggle.

"I'd rather be forty years younger," the other responded.

Eliana smiled and settled back to watch the game. Penny nudged her. "Sounds like we finally have our guy," she whispered. Eliana's smile widened. She fully agreed.

California

Evan walked through the LAX terminal clutching his bag tightly. It all seemed surreal still. Kelly had wanted to come with him, but he had steadfastly refused. She had gotten him here, but from now on it had to be all him. As helpful as she thought she was being, her presence would certainly be a complication.

The director had told him to pack light so his carry-on was all he had as he headed towards the front of the airport. A man holding a sign with 'Garnett' on it caught his attention. He shook his head. What high school teacher got this kind of treatment? He approached the man who led him out to a limo. It wasn't quite what he had expected. Instead of being a traditional stretch limo this was more a really nice luxury car. The chauffeur opened the door for him and loaded the carry-on in the trunk.

Evan didn't know if he should talk with the driver or keep to himself so he decided to watch the sights out the window and follow the driver's lead. The man seemed content to remain silent so Evan allowed his thoughts to drift.

He had honestly been shocked when Eliana had laid the contract in front of him. Surely there were hundreds of men who were a better candidate than him. There wasn't anything interesting about him. Looking the contract over, he found that it had been more generous than he had expected. His mom and sister were positively giddy, and even his dad had seemed content with the idea. Eliana had been beaming happily as she watched him sign. Penny gave a huge sigh of relief. Everyone seemed to think this was the best idea – except for him. So why had he accepted?

With the way everyone else was reacting it was hard to say no. The whole town had been so proud when the news was released. The paper had done a front page spread on him and even a news crew from Des Moines had arrived to do a story about him being on the show. Merryton had given him a big send off although he had disappointed more than one person by not allowing them to give him a parade. His team had teased him relentlessly, but in their eyes he could see the excitement and pride they felt knowing that he would be on the show. Scott had willingly taken over the head coaching duties although the season was nearly over with only the playoffs left. Miraculously the Merryton High School team had barely qualified for the playoffs by one victory.

His mind turned to the upcoming schedule. Eliana had told him that they would leave him alone tonight, allowing him to rest, and explore. He was to stay at a luxury hotel in a suite although he had assured them that a regular room would do fine. Penny had explained that sometimes they ended up having meetings at the hotel instead of at the studio so having the extra space might come in handy. Tomorrow would start the work of production. In the next few days and weeks, there were multiple meetings scheduled, a photo shoot, shopping, and if there was time they would show him where the show was to be shot at.

None of it sounded appealing, but he knew it was part of his job now. Within the next couple weeks there would also be interviews, press releases, and more meetings.

He leaned back in the leather seats of the car and sighed. Silently he began to pray. *Lord, this seems daunting, but to have been selected out of so many applicants, I have to believe this is your will for me. Give me wisdom and strength.* He smiled a bit. *I didn't think I'd be excited over the possibility of finding a wife, but I really am. It's unconventional, but you've used some unusual ways before this.* He thought of Isaac having his wife chosen by a servant based on a sign he had prayed for, of Ruth who had proposed to Boaz in a threshing floor at night, of Esther who was chosen in a beauty competition. That last made him smile. Maybe like Esther he was placed in this position for 'such a time as this'.

The driver pulled up in front of a large opulent building and came around to open his door. He stepped out and thanked the driver when he handed him the carry-on case. The day was warm, and Evan shook his head in disbelief. When he had left home that morning the weatherman was discussing the possibility of snow by Thanksgiving. Now he was glad that he had only worn a light jacket over a t-shirt and jeans.

The foyer of the hotel was magnificent – and much too fancy for someone like him. Marble floors, a large fountain in the center, mirrors and artwork decorating the walls, and a giant ornate chandelier suspended from the ceiling made him feel like he was out of place. The staff was polite and immaculate, but he got the feeling that they were wondering how a backwoods person like him was able to get a reservation.

His suite didn't dispel his feelings of doubt. There was a large sitting room with what looked to be antique furniture. Large windows showed views of a crowded beach. A door opened up to his bedroom which seemed large enough for his football team to stay in although there was only one king sized bed in the middle covered in pristine white linens and more pillows than he knew what to do with. Another door led to a walk-in closet which made him chuckle when he considered the few clothing items he had brought with him. The bathroom had an enormous glass shower with multiple showerheads, a deep, sparkling bathtub, and a separate room for the toilet. A double vanity with marble countertops sat below the mirror and the lighting made everything shine brilliantly.

Evan shook his head again in awe. He seemed very far from Merryton. Kelly would love it. That thought made him pull out his phone and take pictures of everything to send to her. He could almost hear her squeal in excitement. While taking pictures, his attention was caught by a door he hadn't noticed before. It led out to a balcony overlooking both the pool and the ocean. There were a surprising number of people at the pool seeing that the beach was only a few steps away. Then again, maybe he preferred the beach because he was from a landlocked state.

He stood leaning on the railing for a while watching the waves of the ocean until the sun setting on the water reminded him that he should find dinner. When he reached the lobby his face brightened as he recognized someone he knew.

"Eliana!" He crossed the marble floors to meet the director. "What are you doing here? I thought we weren't meeting until tomorrow."

"We're not, but I happen to be staying here as well."

Evan frowned. "For some reason I assumed you lived nearby."

Shaking her head, she said, "I've been traveling so much in the past few years for various projects that I don't have a permanent home. It's just easier to rent a fully furnished place wherever I'm at. But my family does live near here, so you weren't far off."

Evan stuck his hands in his pockets, and enjoyed the feeling of companionship. "I was about to get some dinner. Do you want to join me?"

Eliana hesitated a moment. "Are you certain?"

"As long as we don't discuss work." He smiled. "It's nice to have someone to talk to."

"I can agree to that. Where should we eat?"

Evan shrugged as they crossed the foyer. "I was just going to wander until I found something that looked interesting."

"Do you like Thai food?"

"Probably. I haven't really had any before."

Eliana looked over at him in surprise. "Then I know exactly where we're going to eat." She led him to a small family run restaurant only a few doors down from the hotel. The décor was simple and cheap, which felt more comfortable to him than the opulence of the hotel. She ordered pad thai and a type of curry then split the two plates so they both had a little of each. He felt her eyes on him as he took his first bite. "What do you think?"

"It's good. The curry is spicier than I expected, but it has nice flavor to it."

She smiled at him, pleased that he was enjoying her selections. "So how has your first day been?"

"Surreal. This is like another world – palm trees, ocean, luxury – it's a far cry from teaching high school or a locker room filled with sweaty boys."

"I imagine it is. But not necessarily better." She looked up at him, and he was surprised to see the understanding on her face. They hadn't known each other long, yet she seemed to get how he was feeling.

"Right. I have a feeling that this might be an eye-opening experience for me. Make me appreciate what I already have."

Leaning her elbows on the table, her deep brown eyes searched his. "I think you already appreciate what you have, which is why all the luxury and opulence seems empty. It'll go by quicker than you think."

He smiled. "Thanks. I think I'll be okay. I've already decided to savor the experience and learn whatever God has for me through this."

"That's an excellent way to look at all this." Eliana took a bite of her food. "What most concerns you about this project?"

"Is that work talk?" His mouth twitched.

"No. This is talking about you."

"Which will help you with your job." Her eyes widened. "The more you know me, the more you know what angles you want to pursue during filming."

She couldn't keep back the smile that lit her face. "Not many people pick up on that." She waved her fork at him. "You don't have to answer if you don't want to, but I really do want to know more about you. And not just for the show either."

Evan thought for a moment before sighing. "I guess I'm most concerned about what happens if none of the girls seem right for me. What happens if we hit it off, but they don't want to move back to Iowa with me?"

To his surprise, Eliana didn't have a pat answer designed to push aside his worries. Instead she carefully thought through what he had said. "Well, I suppose that any relationship, whether you meet traditionally or not, has the second issue to contend with, and I think you need to decide whether the relationship is worth pursuing and compromising for, or not. If it's not worth it, then I can't imagine that it would be an enjoyable marriage."

She sipped her water. "As for the first concern, I think that's valid, especially in this situation. You aren't going to get a lot of time with these women. It's possible that there isn't an instant spark of attraction. If not, we'll have you choose the one you feel the most connection with. Afterwards, it'll be up to you if you actually go through with marrying them or not."

"Yeah, but it will be in the tabloids if I choose not to." Evan picked at his food as the pressure washed over him.

"It'll be in the tabloids if you do, so you may as well choose the option that's going to be best for you," she said matter-of-factly. "Knowing you even as little as I do, I know that what's important to you is a marriage that is going to last. It'd be much better for you to deal with the publicity of a break-up, than to go through the publicity of a divorce." She watched him closely before putting her hand on his. "I'll do everything I can to make this process as easy as possible."

Evan nodded absently. "I trust you." He met her eyes. "Or I wouldn't be here."

"Want to go for a walk on the beach?" Eliana smiled softly. "Get our minds off of this stuff, and just enjoy the view for a while."

Just the thought of the ocean waves calmed Evan's nerves. It didn't take long for them to pay the check and get out to the beach. Slipping off his shoes, Evan wiggled his toes in the soft sand. The sun was below the horizon, but there was still enough light on the water causing it to twinkle, the sky a deep blue with only a touch of pink and yellow at the horizon. There were a few brave souls in the water, but nearly all wore wet suits, the Pacific waters being cool at any time of the year, but in November at sunset, it was only tourists who would brave the waters without a wet suit.

"It seems strange that it's nearly Thanksgiving and so warm."

Eliana chuckled. "Californians would disagree. When the sun goes down it's sixty degrees. That's downright frigid."

"I guess there's a lot to learn culturally, too." They began walking along the beach in silence. There were still plenty of people on the sand. Some were lounging with books or chatting with friends. Another group was playing volleyball. Several people used the path to bike, jog, roller blade or skateboard. "It's busy."

Eliana looked around as if she hadn't noticed, and then shrugged. "It's actually not too bad. Come back in July around noon, and you'll see busy."

"Is that an invitation?" Evan didn't know where the question came from, but the answer was important.

"You forget that I never know where I'm going to be at any certain time. For that matter, you don't know where you'll be next summer either. You might fall madly in love with one of the girls from the show and not want anything to do with me."

"Why not? It would be you that helped bring us together."

Eliana smiled somewhat sadly. "I guess so."

"Why aren't you staying with your parents while you're here?" He had been wondering about that since the hotel, but hadn't known how to broach the subject.

Eliana laughed loudly. "My parents have a small home, and while I love visiting, it's not really ideal to stay with them. They already have my two younger brothers still at home plus my abuela and abuelo – grandma and grandpa to you – and recently my aunt moved in with her daughter."

"Wow! Big family!"

"You have no idea." Eliana sighed, but he could tell that she loved it. "I'm the middle of five children. My mom was the oldest of seven. It's her grandparents that live with them now. My father is the youngest of four. All of their siblings had at least three children so when we have a family reunion, it's a big deal."

"Makes my family seem quiet." Evan stopped and stared out at the ocean as the final light from the sun disappeared. "I'd like to meet your family."

"You will." She looked up at him. "I was going to invite you to my family's home for Thanksgiving. It won't be the same as being home, I know, but no one should be alone for the holidays."

"I'd like that." Her thoughtfulness touched him, but it also made him feel more at ease as he realized that she would be taking care of him through the whole process of the show. Somehow he knew that she wouldn't push him beyond what he was comfortable with, and that she would fight for him if anyone else tried to.

Suddenly the idea of the show didn't seem so intimidating. He looked forward to moving the process forward.

Meetings

Bright and early the next day, a knock sounded on Evan's suite's door. Already a morning person, he hadn't even flinched when Eliana had told him that they would be starting before breakfast. A cart was wheeled in by a hotel employee followed immediately by Eliana and Penny.

"Good morning," Penny chirped happily. "Better dig in now while you can." She gestured to the cart which was filled with bagels, cream cheese, fresh fruit, eggs, bacon, orange juice, and coffee. "It's gonna be a busy day."

Taking her own advice she filled a plate. Evan gladly followed her example although his attention was on Eliana who seemed busy on her phone. After a moment she grabbed an apple and a cup of coffee before disappearing onto the balcony. Evan's eyes followed her.

"Don't take it personally," Penny intruded on his thoughts. "Eliana is in business mode. When she's working, she's *working*. There's no down time. But when she surfaces, she's a different person. I think you've already seen both sides."

Evan remembered Eliana's determination when she arrived in Merryton, and the business persona she had when setting up the contract. That memory was quickly followed by the thought of the night before, having dinner with her and walking on the beach. He actually liked both sides. Her business side was impressive, and her personal side was warm.

"I have. She's an interesting lady."

Penny nodded chewing a mouthful of bagel. "She's amazing. Before we know it, she'll be a household name. Her talent won't be long ignored."

Evan felt a surge of pride although he didn't know why. Perhaps it was that his part in the show could help her in her to succeed in her ambitions.

Before long the room was filled with people. Eliana came back in and the meetings began. Schedules were made, details were discussed, things got heated, but Eliana maintained control in a quiet, business-like way. Evan remained silent and was amazed at how much went into producing a television program.

That meeting finished, he was whisked off with Penny to do some shopping. As they entered the limo – the same one he rode in from the airport – Evan asked, "Isn't Eliana coming?"

"No, she needs to meet with some of the other crew members and get things in order. She trusts me for this though." Penny smiled. "Although I won't be surprised if she asks for updates or pictures. She likes to have final approval on everything."

Shopping took forever. Never his favorite pastime, it was nearly torture to spend the entire day trying on clothes, going from one store to the next, with only a break for lunch to intrude on the monotony. It was shocking how much clothing they bought for him – suits, casual clothes, swimsuit, sports clothes – even pajamas. When Penny mentioned underclothes, Evan insisted that he was a big boy and could take care of that himself. The packages would be delivered to his suite, another luxury that Evan had never imagined.

"And now we just need to get shoes," Penny exclaimed gleefully, but Evan stopped in his tracks. A few feet down the street, Penny realized that Evan wasn't following. She turned back around with a questioning look.

"No."

"What?"

"No. I can't go to one more store. It violates every guy code in existence. Please don't make me."

Penny's lips twitched, but she seemed hesitant to give into his request.

He took another tactic. "Call Eliana. Let her decide."

Penny pulled out her phone and placed the call. Evan was surprised at how quickly the call was answered. He watched the pedestrians surging around them simply happy to be stopped for a moment. Suddenly the phone was thrust in his face.

"She wants to talk to you."

Evan's heart sank. He had hoped that Eliana would understand, but apparently not. To his relief, she was laughing when he put the phone to his ear.

"Violates the 'guy code', huh? You're just like my

brothers and father. They get deathly ill if we even mention shopping."

Evan smiled in relief and sympathy. "I'm telling you, there really is a code."

"All right. We can finish tomorrow, but you have to buy shoes."

"Fine." How long could it possibly take to buy a couple pairs of shoes?

"I'm coming to your suite. It's about dinner time. I'll have room service deliver, and we can go through your new clothes so I can decide what shoes we need. That will help the shopping go faster tomorrow as well."

Although he wasn't terribly excited about going through the clothes that had so recently tortured him, the thought of it helping the shoe shopping go more quickly made it worthwhile. "Okay, great." He ended the call and handed the phone back to Penny with a triumphant grin.

"Reprieved – for now," she teased before they turned to go back to the hotel.

It wasn't long after they got into the suite that there was a knock at the door. A waiter came in with a tray of room service. When he revealed the meals, Evan frowned.

"I thought Eliana was joining us." He gestured to the two meals on the cart.

"She is, but I'm not," Penny said, as she grabbed her purse. "Believe it or not, I don't work twenty-four/seven unlike my boss. Unfortunately for you, she thinks you do."

Evan grimaced, but strangely found that the idea of having a dinner alone with Eliana was appealing. He had enjoyed their time last night, and had missed her today. There was a suspicion that he might have even been able to tolerate all the shopping had she been with him.

As Penny opened the door to leave, Eliana bustled in, phone in hand, plopping her purse on the coffee table without looking up. Penny laid a hand on her shoulder to get her attention. "Remember that he's just a man, not a robot. Don't push him too hard or he'll regret that he agreed to this." With that warning, she slipped away.

Eliana smiled at Evan ruefully as she tucked her phone away. "I have been pushing you hard, haven't I?"

Evan shrugged. "I'm willing to work late tonight if it means less time shopping tomorrow."

Eliana threw her head back and laughed. "I'm telling you, you would fit in with the men in my family seamlessly."

The idea made Evan wonder about her family. Would they accept him? Or would he be an outsider? They didn't exactly come from the same background and culture.

Seating herself, Eliana exclaimed, "Let's eat! I'm starving!" She pulled a plate towards her that had a perfectly cooked steak, mashed potatoes (although they didn't have gravy on them like he was used to), and fresh green beans. After a quick prayer they began eating. Evan enjoyed the tenderness of the steak, and the crispness of the green beans. He was even surprised to find that the potatoes tasted good even without the gravy.

"So what have you been up to all day?" he asked between bites.

"Meetings, and more meetings," Eliana groaned. "This is the part I hate. But it's necessary. I'm starting to develop a list of women for you." She grinned and wiggled her eyebrows.

Evan swallowed his bite of steak hard. "Oh, really?" He took a sip of water, his heart pounding. "Any good candidates so far?"

"I'm hoping that all of them will be a good possibility for you, but that's up to you to decide."

He knew it was what he was there for, but the thought of her being so eager to find someone for him sort of stung. "Eager to get me married off, I guess," he tried to joke.

"Well, it's kind of my job." She waved a forkful of green beans at him. "I get paid to do it."

He remembered her telling him that she was hoping to move on from this venture to bigger and better things. "Not for long. You'll be doing more before you know it."

"The only thing I've enjoyed about this project has been meeting you," she replied honestly. Her cheeks tinged pink slightly as if she hadn't intended to be so forthright with him. She stood abruptly. "Are the packages from shopping in your room?"

He looked around. "I suppose so. I haven't really looked for them."

Shaking her head, Eliana opened the doors to the bedroom. "Another part of the 'guy code' I imagine."

"Those things sucked one whole day of my life away. I'm not anxious to look at them again." He followed her into the bedroom and leaned against the door frame as he watched her unpack the outfits. After surveying each one critically, she carefully placed them back in the bags.

"We'll need to get you black dress shoes, brown dress shoes, tennis shoes, sandals, flip flops, cowboys boots . . ."

"Whoa, wait. Cowboy boots?"

She grinned at him. "Definitely."

Groaning, he hit his head on the door frame. "It's going to be a long day, isn't it?"

Eliana seemed to take pity on him. "Tell you what. I'll take you to one shoe store tomorrow – and only one. We'll get everything we need, and then we'll be finished with shopping for good." She frowned looking at the packages. "Did Penny take you to the tux shop to get you measured?"

He slowly raised his head to look at her. Dreading what she might say next, he softly said, "No."

Eliana bit her lips. He suspected that she was trying not to laugh. "Okay, two stores tomorrow and that's all."

"I really need a tux?" The last time he had worn a tux

had been for a college friend's wedding. It had not been an enjoyable experience – hot, stuffy, and uncomfortable.

"It's for the finale. The girls will all wear evening gowns, and you'll be in a tux." Her voice indicated that she understood his reluctance, but that she was firm on this point.

He slumped, crossing his arms across his chest. "Fine." An awareness that he sounded like his football players when they were told to run another drill made the corners of his mouth twitch. Glancing over at Eliana, he saw that she was amused, too.

She walked over to him, placed her hand on his shoulder, and said, "If you're a good boy, I'll take you out for ice cream afterwards." She walked back into the living room and retrieved her purse. "I better get going so that I don't get accused of being a slave driver."

Evan watched her leave, surprised at the disappointment that flooded him. He went out on the balcony. Even in the dark, there were people on the beach. He breathed deeply enjoying the salty air and crisp breeze. If he didn't watch out he'd find that he had fallen in love with the director, and that wasn't why he was here.

Shopping

Eliana was prompt to pick up Evan for shopping. She didn't want to prolong his agony any longer than necessary. The memory of his child-like reaction to shopping made her smile. There weren't many men that she knew that would have tolerated so many stores in one day.

Her knock on the suite door was instantly answered. Evan looked boyish in shorts and an Iowa Hawkeyes t-shirt, his hair was rumpled as if he had run his hands through it recently. She found it difficult to read his expression, as if he were uncertain or guarded, but he smiled and it was gone.

"You ready?" she asked, putting the questions she had about his expression aside.

"Ready to get it over with," he muttered, but the twinkle in his eyes told her he was teasing.

She took him to the largest shoe store she knew. It was a discount warehouse with rack after rack of shoes. With anyone else she would have taken them to designer shoe stores, in fact, they most likely would demand it. She knew that Evan would rather have everything available at once instead of caring about the name of the shoes or the cost. It would help her budget as well which was good because the women would likely be much more expensive.

Evan looked apprehensive at the size of the store. He

glanced over at her questioningly. “I promised you one shoe store. This store has it all in one place,” she explained.

He took a deep breath as if to fortify himself. “Well, let’s get started.”

Eliana found shoes that she felt went with the outfits he had purchased with Penny the day before and brought them over for him to try on. “Comfort is the most important thing. You may be wearing these for long periods of time.”

He seemed to take her seriously, trying on each shoe, walking around, and comparing them with others. When he found ones he liked, he put it in a pile. Once she tried to bring another brown dress shoe after he had placed a box in the stack.

“I already have a pair of those.” He put his hands on his hips.

“But these might be better,” she argued.

“This is going to take forever if you make me try on every pair in the store. I like these ones fine.” His eyes met hers and pleaded. “Please don’t drag this out.”

She smiled and took the box back. His sigh was loud enough that she heard it as she walked away.

In a surprisingly short amount of time they had finished purchasing all that she had wanted for him. At least she thought it had gone quickly. Evan seemed to drag his feet to the tux shop as if he was already exhausted. Maybe he hadn’t slept well or was stressed about the project.

"Are you feeling okay?" she asked.

"What?" He looked at her as if his mind had been wandering. Straightening up, he smiled. "Yeah, I'm fine."

"Tired?" she tried again.

"Just distracted I guess. There's been a lot going on."

She smiled but didn't reply. There had been a lot going on, and it was only going to intensify. Making a mental note to give Evan more time off before shooting started, she entered the tux shop.

"Are you a traditional or modern dresser?" she asked as she looked over the selection of tuxes. "Or perhaps you're more retro?" She pointed to a powder blue suit.

"Um, no. I'd say I'm more traditional." He stopped in front of a black tux with a black bow tie. "James Bond, right?"

"Whatever you need to hear," she replied shaking her head with a giggle. The tailor came over and took Evan's measurements assuring her that it would be ready in plenty of time before the finale.

"That wasn't too terrible, was it?" she asked as they left the store.

"It wasn't pleasant either." Evan smiled at her, and Eliana couldn't help but smile back. She was pleased with Evan more and more every day. He was going to not only steal the hearts of the women on the show, but make his way into homes across the country. Women would love him, and men would admire him.

"Where are we going now?" His question brought her thoughts back to the present.

"I made a promise, and I always keep my promises," she answered as she led him into an ice cream shop. It was a locally owned store that served ice cream made in small batches. There were popular flavors like chocolate and vanilla as well as more exotic flavors such as green tea and honey. The air smelled of fresh baked waffle cones. Small white tables sat around the shop that had pale pink walls and antique signs as decoration. A counter had stools at it giving the feeling of an old-fashioned soda fountain.

Choosing to sit at the counter, Eliana ordered a dark chocolate caramel ice cream while Evan picked a banana split. "This makes up for all the shopping a little bit," Evan teased as he enjoyed his ice cream. "My mom would always bribe me with ice cream when we'd go shopping, too."

"Oh really?" Eliana's eyes twinkled. "Now it's all becoming clear. If you pretend you hate shopping you'll get a reward for being a good boy."

Evan laughed so loudly that he drew the attention of the whole shop. "The hatred was real, but the ice cream made it worthwhile. Although that's not a bad idea." He tapped his spoon against his lips as he thought about it. "So what reward will I get for doing the show? It's turning out to be a lot more work than I expected."

With one hand on her hip, Eliana turned on her stool

to face him. “You’re already getting paid – well, I might add – plus you have the opportunity to meet the girl of your dreams, you get to live in a mansion, have a whole new wardrobe, the engagement ring paid for, dates paid for, and you want more?”

Pushing aside his empty bowl, Evan turned to face her. “Maybe I want some insurance.”

“Insurance?”

His eyes searched her face. Eliana was mesmerized by his soft smile. “How about if none of the girls you pick work for me, you owe me a date?”

Speechless, Eliana toyed with her melting ice cream. “With me? That doesn’t seem like much of a consolation prize,” she finally murmured.

“I don’t agree with you. I think it would be far more than I would deserve.”

Eliana looked up and met his eyes. Even though there was an element of teasing in this conversation, there was an underlying intensity that surprised her. Was he falling for her? That shouldn’t happen! He was supposed to meet twelve beautiful, available women in a short time. Yet a part of her couldn’t help, but be flattered. After all, she had picked him because he was a man she could picture herself falling in love with. What was she going to do?

Releasing a breathy sound that passed for a laugh, she said, “I’ll take you up on that, but only because I don’t think it will be necessary. You’ll find one of the girls irresistible.” With a sinking feeling in her stomach, she realized that he probably would find one of them irresistible. It should make her feel pleased, but instead she felt disappointed.

Shaking the feeling off, she mentally determined that one of the girls on the show would be the girl of his dreams. She had a job to do, and she was going to do it well! “Let’s go,” she said, standing abruptly. “We have another stop to make.”

“I thought you said we’d only go to two stores.”

Eliana’s mouth twitched. She could easily picture Evan as a small boy saying something similar to his mom. “We’re not going to a store. I want to show you something.”

The Mansion

She drove them out of L.A. and into the foothills. Large estates spread out over the landscape. Many of the homes couldn't be seen from the road, tucked behind large walls, hedges, and iron gates. They were opulent, but not welcoming.

Finally she turned into a long driveway. The gates were already opened giving the feeling they were expected. The drive circled around a large fountain with water cascading down the sides. A large, tan adobe building with magenta bougainvillea trailing up the sides stood in front of them. The front door was wooden with black iron decoration intended to make it look older than it was. Balconies of varying shapes and sizes hung off the side.

"What is this place?" Evan said, his voice quiet in wonder.

"Your home for the next month or so." Eliana led him up to the front door and swung it open wide. "Welcome home."

Evan shook his head. "This is not a home. It's beautiful and incredible, but there's no way this will feel like home." He stepped into the high ceilinged entryway with marble floor and a large chandelier. A stairway with wrought iron balustrade curved down from the second story.

"We're going to have you move in this week, get familiar

with the layout, become comfortable with it on your own. You should give the illusion not only to the girls, but to the audience at home at this is your castle, and you are master here."

"I'm just a small town high school teacher," he protested.

"We're not going to hide who you are or what you do, but you should exude confidence in this setting as easily as you do in your classroom or on the football field." She let that sink in before continuing. "I'll take you on a tour."

She led him through a large living room, kitchen, dining room, multiple bathrooms, each one resplendent. As they progressed through the house, she would fill him in on what she foresaw for the show. Bathrooms would be off-limits, as well as bedrooms giving both him and the women a chance to escape and have private moments.

"Down this hallway is where the ladies will stay." She gestured to a closed door on the second floor. "Each will have a sitting room, bedroom, large walk-in closet and a bathroom. I have demanded a rule be instilled that forbids you from entering this wing, and in turn the women are not allowed into your wing." She smiled slightly. "The producers fought me on it. They don't think we will have good ratings if you don't have full access to the women and vice versa. Sex sells and all that, but I think we can protect your reputation and beliefs, and still create a good show. You'll need to help me out on this though."

"What do I need to do?"

“Be open and honest. Treat these women in a way that will make every girl in America wish they had been picked. Try to fall in love.” She pleaded with him earnestly. Her future depended largely on the success of this show, and placing safeguards for him had been risky.

“I’ll do whatever you need me to do.” His sincerity was written on his solemn face, as if he was taking a vow. Satisfied, she turned to move on, but he grabbed her hand. The warmth of his touch was a jolt. She turned back quickly to face him. “Thank you for putting your neck out like that for me. I appreciate that you were willing to stand up for my beliefs so that I wouldn’t be put in an awkward position.”

“No problem. I want you to be absolutely comfortable.” She pulled her hand away and shoved it in the pocket of her jeans. “Let me show you the rest of the house.” She needed to get back to the job, or she was going to forget that he wasn’t there for her.

“House,” he scoffed. “This is more than a house.”

“It is large, but it’s partly because it will tape well, and partly because once the crew shows up, and the women, a lot of this space will be filled. There are more bedrooms that will be for cameramen, caterers, lighting, sound – you name it.”

“Will you be here?”

“In a way. I’ll show you.” They left the house, passed a large swimming pool, a basketball court, tennis court, and putting green before arriving at a smaller house that had similar color and lines to the large one. "I'll be staying here." This building had a smaller, more comfortable feel for Eliana. It had everything she needed – bedroom, bathroom, kitchen, office, living space – in fact, it'd be one of the nicer places that she'd stayed in while shooting.

"Why aren't you staying in the big house?" His gaze roamed the space, and he seemed appreciative, maybe even a little envious of her cottage.

"Honestly, I know I'm going to need some space to think and work. I can't do that when I'm available 24/7. Penny will be staying in the big house though so if something comes up she can handle it." She grinned at him. "She's younger so getting up in the middle of the night for a crisis isn't as difficult."

"Yeah, you're a pretty old lady. What are you? Twenty-five?"

"Twenty-seven."

"That's a nice age." When she scoffed, he continued. "I'm serious. You're old enough to know what you want and how to get it, but young enough to have energy to do it. Unlike me."

"I know your age, and that one year you have on me isn't enough to claim 'old man' status." Eliana led him out of the cottage, locking it up behind her. As they headed back to the main house, she thought again about how Evan was going to win over the nation. He was so much fun to be with, so comfortable to talk to, and not hard on the eyes either. "There is one thing I need your opinion on."

He looked surprised. "I don't know anything about how this works. My opinion doesn't matter."

"Of course it matters. I need you to feel absolutely comfortable. If you're at ease, it'll show up on the screen, but the same thing will happen if you're tense." She stopped near a gazebo and turned to face him. "There are going to be times that you and I need to meet together. I can always bring Penny with me if you'd like a chaperone along."

"We're alone now," he pointed out with a smile.

She flushed. "Yes, but it's going to be different when everyone else is around. We wouldn't want rumors started."

Evan nodded. "I can see your point, but I really don't think it'll be a problem. I don't think we need to make this any more complicated than it already is."

Eliana nodded. "One of the complications we do need to figure out," she said with a smile, "is where we can meet. There's the library or den." Thinking out loud helped her figure things out. She often used this technique with Penny. It was strange that it came naturally to do the same with Evan.

"But the library and den are areas where we may be interrupted since they're open to everyone. Why don't you come to my wing? I've got twenty thousand rooms."

Elbowing him, she teased, "It's only nineteen thousand

five hundred rooms. Stop exaggerating." She frowned as she thought about his suggestion. "I don't think it's right for me to say that your wing is a female free zone, but yet I'm allowed in whenever I want. It doesn't really send the right message."

"Point taken." He leaned on the railing to the gazebo thinking about the issue. Eliana watched him. She loved that he took this seriously even though he had been coerced into applying and had some doubts about the whole project. Knowing him the way she was learning to, she had a feeling that he tackled everything this way. Once a decision was made he was going to do everything he could to make it successful.

Out of nowhere Eliana knew the solution to her dilemma. "Come with me." Crossing the grounds, she led him to a smaller building. Opening the sliding door, she revealed a single room sparsely furnished. A single couch sat on one wall with a mini-fridge next to it. Cabinets and shelves lined one wall while another was floor to ceiling windows. Easels, canvases, paints, and brushes were the clue to what the building was for. "The owner of the home is an artist," she explained unnecessarily. "He's letting us use his home because he's friends with the producer, and he doesn't need it right now while he's in France. What do you think?"

He looked around in apparent confusion. "What makes this place better than the others?"

"It's technically open to everyone. I was surprised that he would allow us to invade his studio, but the producer convinced him that it might work for a date so he capitulated. But it's on the outer limits of the property so we shouldn't be overrun with people who happen to stop by." She shrugged and summarized, "It's private without being off-limits."

"Then it sounds perfect." His face looked worried as he went over to the counter and fingered a paintbrush. "Do you think I'll be able to come up with different dates for each girl? I'm not terribly imaginative."

"These women are all very different. I think that as you look through their applications you'll be able to find something they'll like to do. However, if you're struggling we'll have a couple of consultants who are here to help plan your dates. They will also give you advice whenever you need it."

"Will the consultants be male or female?" Evan moved closer to her.

"Do you have a preference?"

He looked past her out the window. "I can see a benefit to both. A male would be able to meet with me in my private quarters, and would understand that there are some things that just are not 'manly'." He looked back at her with a grin. "I'm sure I'll be doing plenty of girly things. I don't want to lose my 'man card' altogether."

Eliana couldn't stop the giggle that erupted from her. "Okay, I can understand that. So what's the benefit to have a woman?"

"She'll know better what the ladies are looking for." Evan shrugged. "So I guess it's up to you."

Smiling softly, she said, “Well, then I think you’ll be pleased to find out that I have a married couple who are both going to consult with you. She will be allowed into your wing, but only with her husband along. There’s an office space in your wing that will be perfect for you to meet with them. They will also be the consultants for the women as they plan their side of the dates, and then will relay the plans to me so that I can make any arrangements that need to be made.”

They stepped outside, and Evan looked up at the mansion which had a pink glow with the sunset light bathing it. “Will this ever feel normal?”

“I hope not. This isn’t reality.” Eliana surprised herself with that revelation. “This is an illusion that will pass, but hopefully it will result in love that is not an illusion. And that will be worth it all.”

Thanksgiving

Evan hadn't seen much of Eliana since she took him on a tour of the mansion for the show. Penny had stopped by a couple of times to take him to meetings or detail him about some aspect of the show. Once he had asked her why Eliana had all but disappeared.

"She felt like you could use a rest before the show started, and that if she was with you she would probably put you to work. This show is her life right now."

Evan hoped that it was the truth, and that she wasn't avoiding him. Even though he missed spending time with Eliana, in a way he saw the wisdom of her decision. He was able to spend time at the beach, and do tourist things. He even took in a Lakers game at the urging of Kelly. It was nice to relax before what would surely be a very busy time.

More than that though, he was beginning to suspect that more feelings for her than he should – especially since he would be shortly picking another woman with the nation cheering on their favorites. A heavy feeling settled in his stomach as he thought about the pressure of picking a wife from twelve strangers. This wasn't natural – especially for him.

A knock at the door brought him back to the present. Penny stood smiling at him.

"I've been told that it's time to move you over to the mansion. Get packed up!" She came inside and started grabbing things she saw lying around. Quickly he snatched them out of her hand.

"I know this may surprise you, but I'm a grown up and capable of packing my own things. You can call my mom and ask if you're unsure."

Penny laughed. "All right. I'll be out here if you need me" She settled on the couch while Evan went to pack his things.

"Why did they decide to move me now?" He raised his voice so that she could hear him. Eliana had mentioned he would be moving in soon, but he didn't fully understand the shooting schedule. All the meetings and dates were a blur in his mind.

"Tomorrow is Thanksgiving. Early in December the girls will be moving in, and preliminary shooting will take place. Eliana thought you could use some time adapting to your new surroundings without all the pressure of cameras and crew around you." She spoke distractedly as she checked her phone for emails and texts.

Evan smiled remembering that Eliana had told him she had wanted him to have time to know the place before it filled up. It sounded heavenly. To have some time with quiet, time to pray, time to get his heart ready for what lay ahead.

He couldn't believe it was Thanksgiving tomorrow. His mom had already sent five texts making sure he was going to be all right on his own. While he would miss his family, he was certain that he would be fine. Besides he wouldn't be completely alone, at least not if Eliana remembered that she had invited him to celebrate Thanksgiving with her family. He wondered if it would be very different from what he was used to, or if Thanksgiving was the same in California as it was in Iowa. So much seemed different that it didn't seem possible that the holiday would be exactly the same.

Evan zipped his carry-on bag, grateful that all the clothes they had bought on those painful shopping excursions were already at the mansion. Stepping into the living area, he said, "I'm ready."

Penny jumped up off the couch. Her energy always amazed him. It seemed to be boundless. "Let's go."

They climbed in her car. It was a Prius, and Evan was surprised that they both fit with his carry-on as well. It seemed incredibly small to him, and he felt crammed in the front seat.

Penny drove like she did everything else – fast. She weaved in and out of the L.A. traffic with such recklessness that Evan found his fingers clenched tightly around the door handle. To get his mind off her driving, he decided to start up a conversation. "Are you moving into the mansion as well?" He gasped as she narrowly missed a minivan.

"Not yet, I have an apartment and it's not too far away. Once filming starts I will."

"I thought I remembered Eliana saying you would be there." He closed his eyes as she passed a semi.

"Eliana is a slave driver. She won't be content if we don't give one hundred percent, and we can't do that if we actually sleep," she laughed. "Besides Eliana is a wanderer without roots. She doesn't understand that some of us like to be in our own homes."

Evan thought about his place back in Merryton. It wasn't fancy, but it was his. While he enjoyed traveling, he couldn't imagine not having roots. "Do you think Eliana likes it that way?"

Penny shrugged. "I don't know if she likes it per se. It's part of her job."

"So you think someday she might be willing to settle down."

Penny pulled off the interstate into the upper-class neighborhood that he recognized from when he came with Eliana. She glanced at him out of the corner of her eye. "Perhaps, if she met the right guy." He looked over at her quickly to try to determine if she meant something deeper. "Or when she succeeds as a director."

Evan let the rest of the trip pass in silence. Somehow he couldn't picture Eliana being content in his small hometown. Not enough happening or anything exotic to interest a world traveler he supposed. Looking out the window, he tried to envision himself in California, and again he couldn't make the image stick. He was too comfortable in his community, and he liked the Midwest.

In fact, part of why it seemed ridiculous that Thanksgiving was the next day was because of the weather. It was still warm, no changing leaves, and only the autumn decorations in the stores let him know that the holiday was coming. No, California wasn't for him.

The mansion looked even bigger today than it had before. Maybe it was the looming prospect of the show that made it seem that way. He got his bag out, and resisted that urge to kiss the ground at his safe arrival.

Penny pulled out a set of keys. "The front door, your wing, the pool house, and the art studio," she lifted up each key as she spoke, and he tried to find some way to distinguish between each of the pieces of a metal. She plopped the keys into his outstretched hand.

"You're leaving?" There was something different about being in this large home by himself than being in his hotel suite alone. It wasn't that he was scared. It was more that he felt isolated.

"Unlike you, I have work to do," she answered with a smile. "Come to think of it, you do, too."

"What work do I have to do?" Evan actually was glad to have some task to do. Being a gentleman of leisure didn't appeal to him, and he'd been starting to go stir crazy being a tourist all day every day.

"Get settled in. Explore and get familiar with your surroundings. Eliana wants you to feel so comfortable here that it feels like you are the master of this home. You'll be the one to give the girls the grand tour so make a list of what you want to show them and in what order." She opened her car door. "I know it's not exactly coaching, but think of it as making a game plan." With a smile and wave, she tore out of the driveway, her tires kicking up dust on the asphalt.

Evan looked down at the keys in his hand. "Make a game plan," he muttered. "This is unlike any game I've ever played before." Still it was something to do, something to keep him occupied.

He went inside and went directly to his wing. Finding his room, he put his things away. With a notebook and pen in hand, he began wandering around the ground floor, sketching a rough floor plan as he went. He made notes on his page about what he might want to point out in various rooms, or rooms he didn't feel needed to be shown. Again he wondered what these women would be like. Would any of them enjoy cooking and find the kitchen interesting? Any of them enjoy playing games and want to know where to find the game room? Or what about the library? Would any like reading? He supposed Eliana would have a diverse group of women for him to meet.

He was about to sit down with his notebook and make a better plan of his rough notes when his phone rang.

"Hello?"

"You still want to have Thanksgiving with my family?" Eliana asked.

"Yes. Do you still want me there?"

“Sure. But remember my family is sort of big, and loud, and intrusive, and . . .”

“I’m sure it’ll be a wonderful day.” He grinned to himself. “And it’d definitely be an improvement over rattling away in this big house by myself all day.”

“You’re right,” she sighed. “I warned you though.”

“I will keep it in mind, and I won’t hold your family against you.”

“You say that now, but you haven’t experienced them in their full glory yet.” He chuckled, but she continued quickly. “I’ll pick you up at eleven. We’ll eat at noon.”

“Should I bring something?”

Eliana snorted. “Believe me, you don’t need to bring anything. There will be plenty of food. See you at eleven.”

Evan was smiling as he set down his phone. He was beginning to wonder if she had forgotten her invitation. Tomorrow was sure to be an interesting day.

****

Music was blaring loudly already when Eliana pulled up in front of her parents’ house with Evan. She wasn’t exactly sure what his Thanksgivings normally looked like, but she was certain this wasn’t it. The house felt like it was crawling with people. Some of the boys were playing football in the front yard. It looked like it was supposed to be two-hand touch, but was escalating quickly.

“It’s so warm,” Evan commented. “Mom said that snow

was in the forecast already back home."

"Eliana!" A man came out of the house in a t-shirt and jeans. Rushing over, he picked her up and swung her around.

"Miguel! Put me down!" Eliana complained.

"My sister returns and I can't celebrate?" Miguel looked past her and crossed his arms across his chest. "Who's this?" He jutted his chin at Evan.

"I'm Evan Garnett." Eliana appreciated that Evan ignored her brother's rudeness and stuck out his hand. Miguel looked between them before grudgingly taking it.

"Evan is the bachelor on the show I'm directing soon." Eliana watched in amazement as her brother's face instantly changed from protectiveness to welcome.

"Oh! You're a co-worker."

"I guess." Evan's brow furrowed in confusion. "Is that a good thing?"

Miguel laughed loudly. "Hey, Diego! Come meet Eliana's 'co-worker'!" Eliana winced at the loudness of his call. Sure enough, not only Diego responded, but the football game stopped and the house emptied, making the yard feel as if there wasn't a single spot for another human being.

"Uh, hey everyone. This is Evan Garnett. He's the bachelor on the show I'm directing, and he's here far from his family, so I thought I'd bring him by." Eliana turned to Evan. "You'll never remember everyone, so I'll introduce you to only my immediate family. You've met my brother, Miguel. Diego is my other brother. Both are younger than me. This is my father, Juan Miguel, and my mother, Maria. And these are my two sisters, Lupe and Teresa." She moved over to where an older couple stood looking on. Speaking in Spanish, Eliana explained the situation to them, and afterwards they looked at Evan with large grins.

Before Eliana knew what was happening, she was whisked away from Evan into the kitchen while her brothers and dad kept Evan out front talking. She hoped they weren't giving him the third degree.

"He's cute," Teresa said watching Evan out the window.

"I'm hoping that's the reaction most of America will have so they'll watch the show," Eliana said drily.

Lupe checked out her reflection in the mirror. "Do you think I could be a contestant on your show?"

"Absolutely not. It would be unethical, and I don't want you there."

"Now, now, Eliana. Don't be so harsh with Lupe," her mother chided. Eliana struggled not to roll her eyes. Lupe was her mom's favorite – the miracle child, so of course, Eliana wasn't allowed to criticize or say anything that might hurt her feelings. "Maybe you could find a spot for your sister, eh? She'd be a very good actress."

Lupe preened proudly as she turned back to her sister. Eliana stifled a sigh. "Sorry, Mama. It's against the rules for me to select family members for the show."

"What good is having a sister in Hollywood if she won't do any favors for me?" huffed Lupe.

Maria clicked her tongue softly. "Lupe, your sister would help you if she could. But she's not a real director yet."

"Mama!" Eliana complained.

Maria looked up in confusion. "What? I said 'yet'. You'll make it someday, mija." Her mother always softened her backhanded compliments with that term of endearment, me-ha, my daughter.

Teresa was still looking out the window. "But he's single now, right?"

"Teresa! I need him to stay single for the show."

"But that's a few weeks away." Teresa grinned at her sister. "A date or two wouldn't hurt anything."

"Hands off." Eliana sat down at the kitchen counter and put her head in her hands. "I knew I should've taken him to a restaurant for Thanksgiving."

"Bite your tongue!" Maria whirled around to face her. "The girls will behave. Won't you, chicas?" Both of her sisters put on an innocent face and nodded. "See? And we have plenty of food. Being with family is the most important part of this holiday – or any holiday, si?"

"Si," Eliana answered automatically, but unenthusiastically. She had known her mom would raise a fuss if she hadn't shown up for this holiday. She had missed so many lately while she traveled around the world trying to make her name as a director, which her mother had lovingly pointed out, hadn't happened quite yet.

She slipped off the stool and went to look out the window. Smiling she watched as Evan coached her young cousins while they played football. The boys huddled around him, listening intently as he drew up a play. When the huddle broke, the boys took their positions. The snap began the play, and in the blink of an eye, the boys had scored a touchdown. While they cheered, the other side complained. Eliana imagined they were upset because the other team got 'professional' advice. Evan moved across the yard and huddled up with the other team. Another play, another touchdown.

Juan Miguel, Miguel, and Diego chuckled as they watched, but Eliana could tell they were pleased with Evan. It was exactly the reaction she hoped the rest of the nation had to Evan. The girls wishing they were one of the contestants. The men wishing they were him.

Juan Miguel came in. He kissed her on the cheek. "You did a good job picking him. He will do very good."

"Thank you, Papa." Eliana rested in the simple praise. Her father was a man of few words, but when he spoke he meant them from his heart.

Without another word, he patted Eliana on the shoulder and moved towards the back yard. The girls helped their mother, aunts and grandmother finish the meal all of them talking about Evan and speculating about the show. They knew it was a reality show and that it was a dating show, but didn't know the details which were a deep secret. Promos would start today to build anticipation for the show. Eliana said little and let the conversation flow around her while her thoughts wandered to how Evan was doing.

She needn't have worried about him though. By the time they sat down to dinner, Evan had won over the entire family. The smaller boys tried to sit next to him , but were quickly sent to the kids' table. Juan Miguel settled the matter quickly and quietly declaring that Evan would sit next to him and Eliana would sit on Evan's other side. While Juan Miguel didn't say much, when he spoke, the family obeyed.

Everyone situated and the table groaning with food – some traditional American Thanksgiving food and some Mexican food – the family joined hands. "Let us thank the Lord for His many blessings," Juan Miguel said. "Carlos, you start as the oldest child." One by one the children gave thanks for various things – toys, parents, food – then they moved to the adults. Each one gave a blessing until it was Eliana's turn.

"I'm thankful to be home for the holidays this year." The earnestness that flooded her was surprising. Yes her family was large and loud, but it was good to be surrounded by all of them again.

All eyes turned to Evan. "I'm thankful that you were willing to let me join your family for Thanksgiving. It would have been a very lonely holiday if you hadn't." The family cheered and hollered out things like 'you're always welcome here' and 'we're pleased to have you'.

Juan Miguel was the last to go. With a small smile, he looked at each member of the family. "I am thankful that my Savior died for me, and for all of my family." It was the same thing he said every year, and yet every year it seemed to grow deeper in meaning, every year the family hushed as the words washed over them, every year one of the parents murmured their own assent as the year had seen one of their own children accept Christ as Savior. Eliana glanced over to see Evan with his head bowed as if her father had just bestowed a benediction on him.

Juan Miguel continued with a simple prayer for the food, and then the noise level crescendoed again as plates were passed around. Evan leaned over as a plate of tamales came to him. "Does your family make their food spicy?" He kept his voice low.

"Those aren't," she responded, "but I'd stay away from Tio Antonio's salsa. It'll singe your nose hairs if you even smell it."

Evan chuckled. "Fair warning."

The day progressed more smoothly than Eliana could have imagined. Her family welcomed and accepted Evan eagerly. Evan was as charming as ever, and seemed to fit right in. He talked football, teased her brothers, had long discussions with most of her family members, and even broke out his high school Spanish to greet her grandparents.

“He is a good man, mija.” Eliana turned at her mother’s words. “Maybe you should keep him for yourself, no?”

“No, Mama, I can’t. He has a contract to fulfill.”

Maria shrugged. “But you would if you could. I see you watch him all day. It will be hard to watch him all day, every day with other women, mija. Your heart is no longer intact, I think.” She wrapped her arms around her daughter. “I pray the Lord gives you strength.”

Eliana wanted to contradict her mom, tell her that she was mistaken, but the words wouldn’t surface. She had hoped that by giving him space she would remember that he wasn’t there for her, but instead she seemed to be falling even harder for him. As she followed him around all day, she marveled at how well he fit in with her family. She had told herself that her family would hate him, that he would hate the noise, so it wouldn’t work out between them anyway. But as she saw him struggle with his Spanish sitting next to her grandparents, she realized none of that was true.

“What am I going to do?” she moaned to herself.

Shooting

Evan stayed in the shadows of the balcony watching the girls arrive. All of them were lovely, and there were girls of every shape, size, and color. They chatted nervously as they entered each carrying a small suitcase. He figured they were given a new wardrobe like he was so there was no need for multiple bags.

"Lord, how will I know which one is the woman you have for me?" A sudden image of Eliana flitted through his mind, but he pushed it down. Eliana wasn't an option. He had twelve other women to choose from.

"Penny for your thoughts?" A voice startled him. Penny looked up at him and snorted. "Penny? Get it?"

He smiled wanly, and looked down at the girls entering. "Do you think I'll know the right one?"

"Absolutely!" He smiled at her enthusiasm. He should have known that optimistic, romantic Penny would see the show as the perfect way to meet a wife.

"I guess I'm worrying about nothing then."

She shrugged. "I'm not sure about that. It's hard to tell what's going to happen. You know that most reality shows are scripted, but Eliana wants to keep this as unscripted as possible so who knows what will happen." She glanced at her clipboard. "Speaking of that, Eliana wants you to visit wardrobe and make-up, then meet her in the library for your first shoot."

Evan frowned at her. "My first shoot?"

Penny nodded. "Don't worry. It will be like an interview. Eliana will ask some questions, and you answer them as honestly as you can. Piece of cake."

Taking a deep breath, Evan nodded. "Piece of cake."

"Get going!" Penny shoved him. "I've got to go get the girls situated. Relax and be your normal charming self."

Evan honestly tried to relax, but as people surrounded him to make sure that he would look good on camera he felt himself get more and more tense. As the make-up artist whose name he couldn't remember put powder on his face, he closed his eyes and took a deep breath. He could do this. He just needed to remember his game plan. It'd be like coaching a game. Make a plan, run the play, win the victory.

Feeling more confident, he followed an intern to the library where lights and cameras were set up in front of an arm chair. Eliana was in her element in a way he had never seen before. She called out orders and people rushed to obey. Her face was determined and assured. Like him, she had her play all lined up, and as long as her players followed through, she could taste victory.

The intern directed him to the chair and had him sit down. If Eliana even noticed that he had arrived, she didn't let on. He watched her bustle around for several more minutes before finally at a command, the area around him cleared and the room became silent.

At last, Eliana turned her attention to him. Her face was a professional mask with no indication that they even knew each other. With this new version of Eliana, Evan's nervousness increased again. She seemed intimidating and formidable, not like the girl who he had walked on the beach with or spent time with on Thanksgiving.

"This is your introduction to America," Eliana stated. "Start by giving a brief overview of who you are, then I'll ask a few questions. Answer honestly and as concisely as possible please. There's no reason why this should take very long." She sat in a chair near the camera and watched the monitors that had been placed nearby. "On my signal, you can begin. Any questions?"

"Do I look at the camera or at you?"

"At the camera. The viewer should feel like you are talking directly to them." After a slight pause to make sure he didn't have any more questions, she signaled for the crew to begin their routine. Before he knew it, Eliana was pointing at him, directing him to begin.

Evan looked directly into the camera and willed his heart to stop racing. Picturing his parents and Kelly watching at home, he smiled. "My name is Evan Garnett. I'm from a small town called Merryton in Iowa. I'm a high school history teacher and also the football coach." He hesitated, not knowing what else to add.

In a low voice, Eliana asked her first question. "How did you get here?" Evan knew that her questions would be edited out, and only his answers left. It would appear as if he knew exactly what everyone would want to know. Realizing that Eliana wanted to do this interview as quickly as possible, he kept his eyes on the camera and retained a pleasant expression.

"My sister brought the show to my attention, and urged me to apply. I finally agreed, but I fully expected someone else to be chosen. There are many candidates who I'm sure would have been equally as good if not better. I was shocked when they chose me."

The corners of Eliana's mouth quirked letting him know that he answered appropriately. He could barely see her out the corner of his eye, but her presence and reaction had a calming effect on him.

"What do you hope to have happen?" Eliana's quiet voice sobered him. What did he hope to have happen while he was on the show?

"I hope that I will fall in love with a girl who will be my partner in life." He chuckled and shook his head. "It sounds corny, but that's what I want. I want a wife who will stand next to me, support me, encourage me, while I do the same for her. And I hope that out of all these lovely women here, that I will be able to clearly see her, and know without a doubt that she's the one I'm meant to be with." He grinned at the camera. "It would be awesome if a ray of light just lit her up so that I would know this is the one."

Though the curtains were closed in the room, a sudden shaft of light peeked through an opening where the two fabric panels hadn't quite met and lit Eliana up from behind, turning her dark hair into a halo of sorts around her face. Unable to help it, Evan looked away from the camera. Her face had a curious wistfulness to it as if she wanted all the things he had mentioned, but didn't expect to find it. Evan inhaled sharply. She looked so lovely in that light, it was striking.

Abruptly she stood and yelled to cut. "That should do it. Thank you." The crew started to get ready for the next piece on the agenda. Evan stood as Eliana approached him. She smiled distractedly. "That is precisely why I chose you. It was perfect. You're a one-take wonder."

"I'll try to make this as easy for you as possible." A flash of emotion briefly crossed her face, but it was difficult for him to figure out what it was. "So now what?"

Eliana straightened her shoulders. "Now you can go back to your quarters. I'll be interviewing each of the girls. You'll meet them all at dinner tonight. Wear your suit."

She started to move back towards the crew, but he grabbed her arm and pulled her back. "Wait. When will we have time together in the art studio so I can talk to you about things?" He wasn't sure what he wanted to talk to her about, as was made obvious by his brilliant statement about talking about 'things', but he wanted to be able to talk with her whenever he wanted. "Maybe we could have a secret signal for when we need to talk,"

Eliana crossed her arms over her chest, but seemed to consider his idea which was a relief. "What kind of signal?"

Evan's mind raced trying to think of something that would go undetected by everyone else, but that would be obvious to them. "I can put my hand to my chin like this." He put his fist against his chin, his index finger raised and resting on his cheek. "When you recognize the signal you can tuck your hair behind your ear." Reaching out a hand, he tucked a long strand behind her ear. It felt soft and silky in his fingers. He quickly pulled his hand away as if burnt. That hadn't been such a great idea. If he was going to stay focused on the women of the show, he was going to need to avoid physical contact with Eliana.

As if she felt it, too, she took a step back and shook her head. "No, I wear my hair back too often for that to work. The hand on the chin would work, as long as you don't do it without thought. I'll scratch by my ear to let you know I saw your signal. It can work in reverse, too. If you see me scratch by my ear, place your hand on your chin to let me know you got the signal."

Feeling relieved that she had gone along with his plan, he nodded eagerly. "That will work. I guess I'll see you at the dinner tonight."

Eliana nodded and moved off to do her job. Evan sighed heavily as he watched her walk away. He wished they could sit down and talk right then. He wanted to know what had been going through her mind at the end of the interview. Would he ever find out?

Shaking his head at his thoughts, he left the library and headed up to his room. Pulling out the photographs and information sheets, he reviewed the women who were now occupying the mansion with him one more time. Surely one of them would be the one God had for him. There was no reason that he would have been picked from all the applicants unless God had a plan for him to be here. He needed to stop thinking so much about Eliana and start focusing more on the game plan.

Moving to a table with a pad of paper and pencil, he looked over the information again, this time diagramming out his plan of action, making notes, and praying over each one. He knew from past experience that God would direct and that he would be much more likely to see where He was leading if he was diligent about his prayer life.

Dinner

"Everything is all set."

Eliana started when Penny spoke to her. "I'm sorry, what?"

"It's all set." At Eliana's blank look, Penny continued. "The dinner, the girls, Evan – they're ready for you."

"Right." Eliana mentally shook herself. What was wrong with her anyway? She'd never been so distracted during a shoot before. In fact, normally she was laser focused on the task at hand. She knew what she wanted and how to get it.

"Are you all right?" Penny's concern was touching and disconcerting. If the other members of the crew noticed her distraction like Penny had, it could cause problems. She needed them to be able to trust her.

"I'm fine. It's just been a long day, I guess. I'll get some extra sleep tonight and be better tomorrow."

Penny grinned broadly. "I know! I was so excited for the shooting to begin that I barely slept last night. I'll probably sleep like a log tonight."

Eliana smiled half-heartedly and headed towards the women's wing. At least Penny had bought her excuse. Now she only needed to stay alert so that no one else noticed.

The contestants were chatting in the hallway. Dressed up with their hair and make-up done for the cameras and lights, they were all formidably beautiful. Eliana took a deep breath before clearing her throat to get their attention. Immediately the chatter stopped, and only then did she recognize the nervousness these women were exhibiting, and the power she had over them.

"You all know your order so please line up accordingly." There was a slight bustling sound as they hurried to comply with Eliana's order. "One by one, you will go down the stairs. Evan will be waiting for you at the foot. You will introduce yourself by name only then proceed into the dining room. We don't have time for lengthy biographical accounts. You'll each get a turn with him alone, and that's when you can tell him all about yourself."

A tentative hand went up. Eliana nodded to her trying to remember which one this was. Jillian Gosling. The name entered her head finally, and she was thankful that she had a good memory for faces and names. "Yes, Jillian?"

"What if he asks us personal questions at dinner?"

Keeping her face neutral she replied, "You can answer anything he asks tonight at dinner." She bit back the word 'obviously' before it slipped out. These women needed to feel like she was their ally so that they would be willing to obey orders without question. "But try to keep your answers to a reasonable length and not monopolize the conversation."

Twelve heads nodded, anxiety increasing in their

expressions. Stifling a sigh, Eliana tried to ease their worries. "I handpicked each and every one of you because I felt like you had a potential for winning Evan's heart. If I didn't think you had a chance, you wouldn't be here. That said, relax and be yourself. Be the person that I know you to be in order to interest Evan. Don't try to play games."

Several of the women smiled, a few rolled their shoulders back as if relieving a burden, and most seemed to relax. Feeling like she had done all she could do, Eliana reminded them to wait until Penny cued them to begin descending the stairs. Having done all she could for the girls, she went downstairs.

Evan stood in the foyer in a suit looking more handsome than she had ever seen him. She halted on the stairs in midstride when he flashed a smile at her. Heart racing inexplicably, Eliana forced herself to continue the descent.

"You look nice," she mentioned. An understatement if there ever was one.

"Thanks. I'd rather be in a t-shirt though." He smiled. "But my boss won't let me."

"She is pretty demanding." Eliana glanced around noticing that everything was set up exactly as she had specified. They should be able to get a good shot of the girls as they came down as well as get a close up when Evan met each one for the first time. "The girls will come down the stairs one by one and introduce themselves to you. After the last one, you can join them in the dining room for dinner. Try to think of it as a banquet with your football team before the season starts."

"We don't do a banquet before the season. We have training camps."

"Fine, this is training camp. You're not trying to dive deep into their personalities, but rather you want to get a general idea of each girl. Try to get them all to participate in the conversation, and if one is a little too chatty, try to gently steer the conversation elsewhere."

Evan's lips tightened. "Is that all?"

Putting her hand on his arm, Eliana smiled up at him. "Be yourself. You're naturally charming. They'll love you immediately." Realizing she was still touching him, she quickly removed her hand and turned to move into position.

Once the crew was set, Eliana gave Penny the signal to send the first girl down. Eliana didn't have to look at her list on the clipboard nearby to know that this was Sarah Partridge. Her blonde curls bounced as she walked carefully down the stairs, a bright smile on her face revealing her endearing dimples. She was the 'girl next door' type. A simply cut ice blue dress made her blue eyes pop. Eliana shifted in her seat to see what Evan's reaction was.

He was smiling politely, but there was no mark of instantaneous attraction. Sarah approached and shook his hand, introducing herself. He murmured a courteous response, and then she was off to the dining room.

Next was Paloma Valdez, a distinctly different type

from Sarah. Paloma was slender with long black hair, brown almond shaped eyes, and full lips. More of an exotic beauty and her hint of a Spanish accent only added to that impression. Wearing a form fitting red dress certainly helped her stand out as well.

Again it was difficult to read anything other than polite interest as Paloma introduced herself to Evan. One by one the rest of the women came down. Eliana found that she watched Evan more than the women, holding her breath at his reaction to each one. She didn't want to probe too deeply, but she suspected that she more dreaded seeing him light up with attraction than hoped for it. What kind of director was she to not want what was certain to get interest from viewers?

When the final contestant went into the dining room, the crew immediately began tearing down to move into the dining room for the next segment. Evan approached Eliana hesitantly as if afraid to be in the way.

"Am I supposed to go in right now?" he asked gesturing towards the dining room.

"No, wait here. We'll want a shot of you entering the room. It seems to take forever for us, but on TV it will appear to happen directly after the last lady entered." She stuck her hands in the pockets of her jeans feeling underdressed for the occasion. "What's your first impression?" She couldn't help the question, but her eyes followed the activity around them instead of looking at him.

Evan shoved his hands in the pockets of his suit almost

imitating her. “They’re each very different, and all very lovely.”

Eliana nodded. She hadn’t known if he had a type of woman he was attracted to so she had been looking for diversity in looks as well as personality when searching for contestants. The list had been immediately approved by the producers which told her that they thought these women were all beautiful as well. “They’re each different in personality as well. I wasn’t sure who you might be drawn to so an eclectic group gave me the best chance of finding someone you would click with.”

“Do you have a favorite?” he asked. “Someone you particularly think I’ll be drawn to?” She felt him look at her.

Shaking her head, she bit her lips. “Like I said, I don’t know your type.”

Eyes still on her, he shifted ever so slightly towards her. “I’m not sure I have a type. I do find myself drawn to strong, capable women who know how to lead. Someone with a dream that they’re not afraid to go after. A woman who gets the job done and done well with confidence.”

Eliana inched slightly away. “There are several women who would fit that description. I think you’ll be fine.” Then she hurried away, afraid to read too much into what he had said.

Penny found her in the dining room. “Did he seem to favor anyone yet?” she asked eagerly. “I couldn’t really see from where I was.”

"No, he was polite with each one, but no sparks seemed to fly."

Penny's face fell briefly, but she quickly brightened. "That's okay. I have a feeling he'll pick Emma Laird." She nodded to the pretty woman with dark brown hair and emerald green eyes. Emma had an athletic build and had chosen a deep green velvet dress that softened her muscular form.

"Why do you think he'll pick her?" Eliana shoved aside the initial burst of jealousy that filled her.

"They're both athletic, and they're both from Iowa. Seems like they'll have a lot in common." Penny shrugged. "Who do you think he'll end up with?"

Eliana searched the faces of the women who were chatting with one another. "I honestly think he could be happy with any of them." The words dampened her spirit because it was the truth. Any of these women could make Evan a very happy man. She forced her mind back to the task of setting things up for the next segment in order to keep her spirits from sinking low. Most importantly she didn't want it to be obvious that she was struggling with this assignment. This was supposed to be her big chance to prove to some of the high powered producers that she was capable of fantastic things. Getting emotional would not help her cause.

"Well, sure he could be happy with any of them," Penny interrupted her morose thoughts. "But don't you have one you're pulling for?"

"I can't do that. These women need to know that I don't favor one of them over the other, that I will give them equal opportunity and won't edit the film to make them appear worse than the others. I need them to trust me." And with that, Eliana promised herself that she would do exactly that. No matter how hard it was, she would make sure that Evan got to see each woman in the best possible light, and to never let her feelings or emotions taint them either to Evan or to the viewers.

It seemed to take a long time, but finally the next segment was set. Eliana realized that everything had been switched with incredible efficiency although she doubted it felt that way to the women or Evan.

As she got ready to signal the start, the women sat up straighter and looked towards the door Evan would enter. The cameras began to film, and Evan was cued to enter. He came in looking very much like he was completely at home, and was master not only of the house, but of the situation as well. Eliana was proud of him as she listened to him interact with each of the ladies through the elegant meal. He made the shyer women feel comfortable, and asked intelligent questions. When they asked him questions, he gave them honest and straightforward answers.

"Do you really think you'll fall in love in such a short amount of time?" asked Robyn Talbott, an African American business woman. Eliana smiled at her blunt question. It was nothing less than what Eliana would have expected from the no-nonsense woman. Even at the dinner, Robyn had dressed in a black skirt and matching jacket over a white blouse. Her outfit did make her stand out from the brighter colors around her.

Evan set down his fork and looked her right in the eyes. Eliana could tell he was thinking through the question and his answer carefully. “I don’t know. I’m praying that God will lead through the process, and that I will be able to fall in love with one of you.” His glance swept the table and the girls each smiled back at him, hope written clearly on their faces. He turned back to Robyn. “Do you think you could fall in love with me in such a short time?”

Robyn smiled broadly as he flipped the question back to her. “I think half of us are already pretty smitten.”

As Eliana glanced around the room, she realized it was true, and it wasn’t only the contestants who were showing signs of falling for Evan. The women on her crew were hanging on his words as well. It would be easy for any of them to want to choose to be with him. So far though, he gave no indication that he was drawn to one of them over the others. Would it be possible for him to leave the show without falling for one of the women?

She looked over the group at the table again critically. Shaking her head, she realized that it wasn’t likely that one of them wouldn’t attract him. These were not only women who were lovely to look at, but they had lovely personalities as well.

Holding up his water glass, he said, “To all you lovely women, I wish you the best of luck, and I look forward to knowing you better.”

They raised their glasses with him, some of them clinking theirs against their neighbors. Evan set his glass down and put his chin on his hand, while he listened to his neighbor. Eliana frowned wondering if it was the signal they had set up or simply absorption in the conversation. Then Evan's eyes looked directly at her letting her know that it was for her. She scratched by her ear, and he turned his attention back to the conversation. Eliana smiled to herself. She was looking forward to talking things over with him after they were finished for the night.

Conversation

Evan let himself into the art studio and turned on the light. It wasn't surprising that Eliana hadn't made it yet. She had a lot more work to do than he did.

After the dinner he had changed into workout shorts and a t-shirt and felt much more comfortable. Thinking back over the dinner, Evan frowned as he stared out the window toward the lighted windows of the mansion. Eliana had done an excellent job of choosing women. He had actually been surprised at how easily the conversation had flowed. There didn't seem to be any tension between the ladies – at least not yet. He actually was looking forward to his dates for the first time since he had signed on.

And yet . . .

All during dinner, he had fought the urge to look over to Eliana. He had wanted to include her in the conversation at dinner. Even in jeans and a casual top, she had rivaled the rest of the women in beauty. Why was he most attracted to a woman he couldn't have? He had twelve lovely, intelligent, accomplished women to choose from, but he was drawn to the director.

The sliding door opened and he turned around. Eliana smiled apologetically as she entered. "Sorry it took so long. I had to get things wrapped up from tonight and make sure everything is set for tomorrow."

"I understand. I wasn't surprised that I got here first." He took a seat on the couch, and gestured for her to join him. He smiled as she took a seat as far away from him on the couch as she could. "I won't bite."

"I know, but if anyone were to happen by . . ." She gestured to the large windows. The studio might be private, but there were no curtains and with the lights on they could clearly be seen if anyone came around.

"You're probably right." He raked his fingers through his hair. "Are you used to living in a fish bowl?"

She laughed softly. "I would think you would be, living in a small town as the high school football coach."

He smiled ruefully. "I guess it feels different. There I'm in a fish bowl with people I know and love. Here I'm in a fish bowl with strangers."

"You did a wonderful job tonight. The women are already eager to spend time with you. Robyn wasn't far off when she said that many of them are half in love with you already." Eliana looked down at her feet. "How do you feel about tomorrow?"

"Surprisingly, I'm feeling kind of excited about the possibility. Sarah seems like a nice girl, and I think we'll have a good time." He rubbed his hands together absentmindedly. "It is Sarah tomorrow, right?"

"Right," Eliana smiled looking up at him. "Do you have your game plan all ready to go?"

"It's ready. I think after tonight I might alter some

things. It's different seeing the competition on paper and seeing them in action."

Eliana raised an eyebrow. "I'm not sure they would appreciate being seen as competition."

He chuckled. "Sorry. I guess I'm stuck in my football analogy. Maybe I should say it's different seeing a new recruit on paper and in person."

"That's probably a little more appropriate." Eliana stood and started pacing the small space. "Do you have any questions for me?"

Evan stood and watched her move restlessly. She probably still had work to do tonight, and he was keeping her from finishing. "You probably have things to do."

Eliana stopped and looked at him, crossing her arms across her chest protectively. "I do, but if you have something you wanted to discuss, I'm always available for you." She bit her lip and looked away as if wondering if she should have said that.

He tried to hide a smile, but his heart beat wildly at her words. Something in him needed to know that she would be walking with him through this. "I'm glad to know that," was all that he ended up saying.

"You were the one who asked to meet tonight," she reminded him.

Stepping closer to her, he took a chance and did what he'd wanted to do for a while. Cupping her chin he slowly lowered his head giving her ample opportunity to back away. She drew in a breath and closed her eyes. That was all the encouragement he needed. Gently he put his lips on hers. His heart raced at the soft warmth of her mouth under his own. Too soon he pulled away and looked into her eyes.

"I've wanted to do that all night," he whispered, his hand still caressing her face.

She pulled back slowly as if reluctant to end the contact. "Right. With all those beautiful women dressed up so lovely you wanted to kiss me." The doubt in her eyes hurt him.

"It's true. I fought wanting to watch you, talk to you, all night long."

"What are you doing, Evan?" Eliana shook her head, her face was flooded in confusion. "You have twelve dates to go on – and none of them are with me. You have to make a choice by the end with one of those women back in the mansion. This is not going to help anything."

"You're right, of course, but I needed to know what it would be like to kiss you just once before all the craziness starts. I promise it won't happen again." He reached out for her, but she stepped back. "Didn't you feel it too, though? Didn't it feel like it was right?"

Eliana closed her eyes before shaking her head. "It doesn't matter. It can't happen. Not now."

Without another word, she crossed the room and left the studio. He stood at the window watching her hurry across the property to her guest house quarters. His head fell. Had he ruined everything with his impulsiveness? It had potential to ruin his chance with Eliana and also ruin his chance of finding a wife among the women in the show, because now he knew just how powerful a kiss could be.

The 1st Date

Pre-date interview with Sarah Partridge

"I'm excited for this date, but it's a lot of pressure, too. By the time he gets to pick at the end there will have been eleven other dates. Mine has to be extremely memorable for him to remember me." Sarah flashed a bright smile right at the camera. "Fortunately, I think I have the perfect date planned."

Eliana struggled to not roll her eyes. "Cut!" she hollered. "That was great, Sarah. You can go get prepared now." Eliana rubbed her forehead as the bouncy blonde left.

"Are you all right?" Penny came up beside her, a concerned expression on her face. "You're not getting sick are you?"

"No, I'm fine. I just didn't sleep well." She left out the part that it was because of a mind-blowing kiss that she had slept so poorly. No one could ever know about that kiss, and yet she couldn't stop thinking about it.

Now Evan would be going on dates with other women, possibly even kissing them. A surge of jealousy rushed through her, but she quickly pushed it down. She couldn't afford to be jealous of these women. Both her personal well-being and her professional career depended on her being able to focus on the task at hand.

"We need to get Evan's pre-date interview," she reminded Penny, trying to keep her mind on the job instead of the man.

"He's ready for you," Penny responded. "He seems like he didn't sleep so well either. Kind of cranky, which isn't like him at all."

When they entered the room, Evan was pacing, looking agitated. He stopped when he saw her and rushed over. Looking around to be sure no one was near, he said, "About last night . . ."

"I don't want to talk about it. We have a job to do." Eliana's words were curt, and Evan jerked back as if she had slapped him.

"If that's how you want it." He shrugged, but she could tell he was hurt.

She kept her voice low. "Look, Evan, it's not how I want it, but it's how it needs to be. You see that, right?"

He nodded, then raised his chin defiantly. "I don't regret it," he said with in a soft voice. "If I could go back and change it, I wouldn't." Eliana's heart raced even as she tried to keep her facial expression neutral. "I needed to know what it was like to kiss you before I started this process. I feel like I can make a much better decision now that I've experienced that." That said, he went and sat in his chair, preparing to give his interview.

Eliana sighed deeply. How was she going to do this?

Shaking herself, she took her spot by the monitors and

gave the directions to begin filming. Penny prompted Evan with some questions, while Eliana watched the monitors.

"I'm excited and nervous all at once," Evan said with an endearing smile. "I have no idea where this journey will lead, but I know that I've already grown." He looked right at Eliana. "There are things that have already happened that may have changed my life forever."

Eliana bit her lip. He continued through the interview, but she barely heard a word of it. When he finished, Evan left without another word, and Eliana was glad for the reprieve.

After giving directions to the crew about where and how to set up for the first date, Eliana slipped into an unoccupied room and took a deep breath. "Lord, I'm giving this day to You now. I can't do this alone. I don't know how or why it happened, but I think I've fallen in love with Evan. God if it's Your will it will work out. And if it's not Your will then I don't want it either. Keep my focus fixed on You alone." Feeling stronger, she left to face the first date.

******

Evan stood in the foyer of the mansion waiting for his first date to arrive. He had read up on Sarah Partridge last night until he felt like he knew her better than he knew himself. She was cute, had a bubbly personality (he had noticed that at the dinner), loved the outdoors – on paper she was a good fit for him, but he didn't feel any excitement about spending time with her. Of course, part of that might be due to the fact that he would much rather spend time with the director than any of these women.

He glanced over at Eliana who was talking animatedly with a cameraman. She wore jeans, a t-shirt, and a baseball cap with her dark hair pulled into a ponytail. He was certain that Sarah would look more glamorous, but couldn't imagine that she would be lovelier than Eliana.

Straightening his shoulders, Evan pushed the thought aside. Eliana needed him to give this his best shot. If nothing else, he needed to give the illusion of enjoying his time with these women. It was acting. Acting? What did he know about acting? He was a football coach. Okay, stick to the game plan, and that plan included giving each woman a fair shot.

"Okay, we're set!" Eliana called out. "Places!" When she called for the action to begin, Sarah came down the stairs, a bright welcoming smile on her face. She wore designer jeans with boots, and a plaid button up shirt. Her blond curls framed her face, and the blue in her shirt brought out her baby blue eyes. She was 'girl-next-door' cute with dimples and big eyes.

Evan waited for her at the bottom of the stairs. He was also in jeans and boots, but wore a t-shirt and a baseball cap. He had been told that Sarah had planned for them to have an outdoor date, but not exactly what it was.

"I'm so glad to have our date today," she said with a giggle. "It's going to be so much fun!"

"I'm looking forward to it as well. Where are we going?"

"It's a surprise!" She giggled again. He forced a smile. If she was going to giggle throughout this date, it would get old really fast.

"Can't wait." He led her out the door. Together they climbed in a car that Sarah drove. They chatted on the way, Evan was aware of the dash cameras that were installed to catch all of their conversation. It was just small talk, but it was pleasant. Most of what they discussed was on the forms he had already read through a dozen times, but he realized that the viewers didn't have the same access. They talked about how she had graduated from Washington State University with a degree in agriculture. Her family owned a pear orchard, and she had always known that she would be part of it when she grew up.

Finally they arrived at a picnic spot in the mountains with pine trees surrounding them, a stream trickling nearby. Cameras were already set up to catch the moment they arrived. Eliana stepped out the car that had been following them up. Evan made a point of keeping his attention on Sarah although it was hard.

Sarah got out a blanket and a picnic basket from the trunk of the car. "I love picnics. We have picnics under the trees in the orchard all the time back home."

"Gotta admit that back at my home we're not able to have picnics at this time of year," he said with a warm smile. "In fact, my sister told me they'd had snow this week."

"It doesn't snow too often in Washington, although it's too cold there for a picnic, too." She spread the blanket by the creek and started unpacking the basket. There was fried chicken, a pear salad, fresh pears, and a cake that seemed to have pears in it as well.

Evan was glad he liked pears, but that much in one sitting seemed like a lot. "Are these from your orchard?"

Sarah's face beamed with pride as she nodded. "I had my parents send some down especially for today."

They sat down on the blanket and began to put food on plates. Evan couldn't help glancing at Eliana. Her face was expressionless as she watched the date unfold, quietly giving instructions to those near her.

Evan picked up a pear and looked at the sticker on it. *Partridge Pears* was written on the sticker with a small picture of a partridge in a pear tree. Evan cocked his head to the side as he looked at the sticker again. "A partridge in a pear tree?" His voice was soft, but Sarah was so close she heard him.

"Yep. Clever isn't it? Since we are Partridges after all." She giggled again.

Evan looked at Eliana and placed his hand on his chin. "That is clever."

Eliana narrowed her eyes, but reluctantly scratched by her ear signaling that she had received his message and would meet him later. Evan turned his attention back to Sarah.

He kept her talking about herself – a subject she was happy to share. In fact, she was eager to chatter, and he soon found that he didn't have to do much other than nod to keep her going. Over Sarah's shoulder, he saw a member of the crew nodding off, and stifled a smile. If this was going to be entertaining television, he'd better do something else quick.

Holding Sarah's hand, he gently raised her to her feet. By the goofy smile on her face, he realized that the simple touch had given her hope in something deeper. Quickly he dropped her hand. "I think we should be going back if we're going to be ready for our evening date."

She looked disappointed, but then lowered her eyelashes demurely. "What are we doing tonight?"

"It's a surprise," he parroted. They cleaned up and started the trip home with Sarah chattering on the whole way.

When they arrived back at the mansion, Eliana grabbed his arm as he started to follow Sarah inside. "What are you doing?" she asked in exasperation.

"I'm getting ready for a date."

"No, what are you doing allowing her to dominate the conversation? This is boring." Eliana huffed and took a couple paces away from him. "I don't even know if I can edit this to make it interesting."

"What do you want me to do?"

"Be more involved. Talk about yourself sometimes. The viewers are going to want to know who you are!" Eliana sighed. "Are you even trying?"

"I am! I promise. I know how important this is to you." He took a step towards her. "But were you actually trying to pick women that I would be interested in, or just trying to be cute?"

"What do you mean? Sarah is a lovely girl."

"Yes, she is. A bit on the giggly, self-absorbed side, but she's cute enough. I'm talking about the Partridge Pears." Eliana's face didn't reveal anything so he continued. "On the first day of Christmas my true love gave to me a partridge in a pear tree. Sound familiar?"

Eliana's lips started to tilt up in a smile. "Can't I have tried to be a little cute and still think they were good potential candidates for you?"

Evan groaned. "Are they all this way?"

"Chatty, giggly, and self-absorbed? No."

Closing his eyes, Evan knew he had his answer. "They all have to do with the lyrics of the Christmas song don't they?"

"Maybe," Eliana said reluctantly. "I promise you that I really did think that they might be someone you would be interested in. The rest was for fun."

"What did you think I'd see in Sarah?"

Eliana shushed him. "Keep your voice down. Do you want rumors going around already that you're not interested in her? And how will she feel if someone tells her that you couldn't believe she was even chosen?"

He glanced around, and lowered his voice. Maybe Sarah wasn't his type, but he didn't want her to be hurt either. "So what was it you saw in her?"

Eliana folded her arms around her middle, tilting her head defiantly. "She's cute, fun, smart, and loves living in rural areas. It wasn't too far out of the realm of possibility that she would be a good match for you. Plus I think she's nervous which is making her extra chatty."

Evan put his hands on his hips and stared off into the distance. He didn't want to admit it, but he could see why Eliana had chosen Sarah in spite of her flaws. "All right. I'll try to take more control of the conversation tonight."

"Thank you." Eliana moved towards the mansion, and Evan wondered if he would get through the night.

Wearing dark slacks and a blue shirt, Evan guided Sarah onto a boat. The sun was sinking in the sky, but there was still plenty of light to see how her light blue sequined dress brought out her eyes.

"I feel like I should apologize," she began. "I realized how much I monopolized the conversation this afternoon. I'm so sorry. I can get that way when I'm nervous. Just stop me when I start chattering on randomly, it's okay . . ."

He laid a hand on hers to get her attention. "It's okay. I should be more assertive."

She smiled in relief. Looking out over the edge of the boat, she sighed. "This is beautiful."

"I know you like being outdoors, and that you have fond memories of the ocean from summer trips to the coast with your family."

Sarah smiled shyly. "You know me well. How about you? Do you like the ocean?"

Evan smiled drily. "I don't get the chance to see the ocean often since I'm in the middle of the country, but I enjoy time on the lake." He looked out at the sun shining on the water as it neared sunset. "I have to say that it's beautiful here though."

A waiter came and served them dinner at a table set for two, while a violist serenaded them. "It is beautiful," she said softly.

"No pears with dinner though," he teased.

Her face flushed slightly, but she took the jest in stride. "I don't blame you. That was a lot this afternoon even for me."

"They were some of the best pears I've eaten." He didn't need to exaggerate. They had been perfectly ripened and were sweet and juicy. "I'm glad you wanted to show me the fruits of your labors - literally." He smiled at her and she blushed.

Conversation through dinner was more balanced with them discussing his football team, history, teaching, and his family as well as more about her life in Washington. He could visibly see Eliana relax as the date progressed.

The sun set, stars came out and lights turned on the

boat. As the violinist played, he asked Sarah to dance. She eagerly came into his arms, and he was surprised to realize that he was enjoying himself. Sarah rested against his chest, and was surprisingly quiet.

"I thought I'd ruined my chances with that disaster this afternoon," Sarah admitted softly, "but you've been wonderful to me this evening even though I probably deserved for you to make this the shortest date in history."

He glanced over at Eliana. "I realized that you were chosen because you have some endearing traits, and that I should give you a fair chance."

Even with her head against him, Evan could tell she was smiling. "I'm glad you did." She pulled away. "Even if you don't choose me, I know that I will remember tonight for the rest of my life." She smiled broadly. "Although I will try hard to forget my behavior on my afternoon date with you."

Evan smiled in sympathy. "I'm guessing before this is through, I will have moments like that myself."

As they entered the mansion, Sarah looked up at Evan, her blue eyes wide. He knew she was hoping for a kiss good night, but with his memory of kissing Eliana he couldn't make himself do it. He pulled her into an embrace and softly brushed his lips against her cheek.

With a small flicker of disappointment in her eyes, Sarah smiled softly, and moved into the room for the post-date interview. Evan sighed and ran his fingers through is hair. Eleven more to go! He had no idea that it would be so exhausting.

He went to the library to prepare for his own after date interview. Penny eagerly came up next to him and asked, “How did it go?”

“It went well. I think Sarah is a lovely girl, and I’m glad I had the opportunity to know her. I’m not sure we clicked right away, but I will definitely not forget her.”

Sarah Partridge’s post-date interview

“Evan is a gentleman through and through. I don’t think I made the impression I was hoping for, but I can guarantee I won’t be lost in the crowd.” She smiled, but not as brightly as she had at the beginning.

Eliana sighed as she watched her disappear up the stairs, and even felt sorry for her. It hadn’t been a stunning first date, but it would be memorable. Now she only needed to work with the editor to make sure that it was not insanely boring.

The 2nd Date

Pre-date interview with Paloma Valdez

"I am looking forward to taking Evan to see my favorite place in the whole world," Paloma's voice had a trace of an accent that went with her exotic beauty. Her long black hair and deep brown almond shaped eyes looked lovely on her tanned skin, and her full lips only added to her good looks. "I'm fortunate to be able to work every day in this location, and I can't wait to give him a tour that he will never forget."

Eliana watched the interview critically. Not only was Paloma absolutely beautiful, but she was intelligent, and poised as well. Where Sarah was chatty under pressure, Paloma looked regal and in full control.

******

Evan waited in the foyer for his second date with a sense of trepidation. After the disaster with Sarah, he wasn't holding much hope that any of the dates would be successful. Maybe that made for better TV than for things to go well, kind of like how people can't look away from a car accident.

He hadn't heard Eliana's call for filming to begin since he was immersed in his own thoughts, but he was aware of a stir among the crew. Men stood a little taller, and an excitement buzzed through the air. Looking up, he saw Paloma coming down the stairs. She was dressed in skinny jeans, tall black boots, and a bright red sweater. He had of course met her at the dinner, but had forgotten how beautiful she was.

"It's great to see you again," he said, eagerly extending his hand.

She took his hand and shook it firmly. "I'm looking forward to our day together."

Again they got in the car with Paloma driving, but instead of a short drive, she headed for the interstate to San Diego. "Have you ever been to San Diego?" she asked as she merged onto the interstate.

"No, I haven't. Is that where you're from?" He already knew the answer and had a good idea of where they were heading, but knowing that the viewers would not have the same background information he had, he asked anyway.

"I am, although originally I'm from Florida. My parents came over from Cuba, and we spoke Spanish in my house all my life." Her accent was faint, but he had still picked up on it. "But I love San Diego more than Miami." She smiled over at him.

"I've always wanted to go to San Diego, but haven't seemed to be able to make it there somehow." Evan watched the passing scenery.

"It's much nicer than L.A. Still crowded, but feels more – I don't know – laid back."

"I like laid back." He thought of Merryton and was

struck with a feeling of homesickness. The town square would be decorated for Christmas. It was one of the few towns left with a nativity in the decorations. Snow on the ground, The Ground Floor busy with people warming up with a cup of coffee, and Christmas carols playing everywhere would contribute to the cheerfulness of the season.

As if reading his mind, she said, "Do you miss your home?"

"At times," he admitted.

"Have you given thought to what happens after the show?" When he didn't answer right away, she continued. "All of us have our lives, our homes, our families, our jobs – it might not be so easy to simply pack up and move to Iowa." She glanced at him. "Are you prepared to make changes if necessary as well?"

Evan had already given thought to that as well, but he weighed his words carefully. "I know that for some of you moving to Merryton might not be terribly difficult, but for others it would be a huge, life-changing event. For example, asking Sarah to leave her family's orchard would be a difficult decision. I've thought about whether I'd be willing to move if it came to that. Honestly, I can find another teaching job somewhere else, so even though I love my hometown, I would be willing to consider moving if the woman I loved needed me to."

He could tell that Paloma was pleased with his answer, and he understood. Paloma's job was a dream job in her field. Moving to Iowa would be a giant step down for her career. What he left out was that he hoped to one day to be able to coach college football. If that opportunity arose, he would hope that his wife would be willing to make the same sacrifice for him.

Paloma pulled into the employee entrance of the San Diego Zoo. She turned to him excitedly. “Welcome to the best zoo in the world – in my humble opinion.”

They climbed out of the car. Evan realized that he was quickly becoming so accustomed to having the cameras around that he barely noticed them. Paloma guided him to the entrance and used her badge to get them inside.

“I’m a veterinarian here,” she explained. “I got permission to give you a backstage tour.” She showed him the medical facilities, the kitchen where food was prepared for the animals, and the educational spaces before leading him out to see the animals.

“So do you have a favorite animal?”

Paloma smiled broadly. “I’m a sucker for the reptiles. When other little girls wanted a kitty or a puppy, I wanted a turtle, a snake and a lizard.”

“All three?” Evan chuckled.

“All three and more. But turtles and tortoises are my very favorites. My first pet was a box turtle named Shelly.” She shrugged. “Unimaginative, I know, but I was five. There’s something about their slow movements, their wise faces, their shells that I find endearing.”

“So is there a tortoise or turtle here that is your favorite of all the animals?"

Smiling, she led him quickly to where the Galapagos tortoises live. Pointing to a large one, she said, "That's Gerty. He was a movie star. There is a scene in the 1941 movie, *Malay*, where you can see him. However, he hasn't let his celebrity status go to his head." She laughed softly. "They're such peaceful animals."

He had to agree with her there, although he preferred animals that were a little more active. His favorite part of their trip was the cheetah talk. Seeing a cheetah on a leash was a surprise, but he loved watching the slender cat with long legs built for speed.

As they left, he thanked her. "The San Diego Zoo was always on my list of places I wanted to go 'someday'. I never expected to get such an intimate look at it."

"I love to share my passion. The animals always amaze me." She led him to the car. "So now where do we go?"

"Now it's my turn to drive," he said with smile, holding out his hand for the keys.

******

Evan waited in the hotel lobby. Knowing they would need to change clothes before the evening date, his consultants had set up a space at a nearby hotel. He had expected that it would take longer for Paloma to get ready than it would for him so he brought a book about World War II along with him to read while he waited.

Someone sat down next to him. "It's going better

today." He glanced up to see Eliana next to him.

Closing his book, he smiled at her, glad for a moment alone. "It is. Paloma is beautiful, smart, and easy to talk to."

Eliana nodded, but kept her eyes on the floor. "She's practically perfect."

He shrugged. "Maybe." He touched her cheek turning her face to him. With a soft voice he said, "But she's still not you."

The pleasure in her eyes was unmistakable before she turned away. "You still have one more date with her."

They both stared for a while at the people crossing the lobby, and yet he felt like they were the only two there. "Do you honestly think Paloma would give up her dream job at the zoo if I were to get my dream job of coaching college football somewhere else?"

Eliana considered his words, then slowly shook her head. "Only if there were another large, prestigious zoo in the vicinity."

"That's what I thought, too. And the chances are that my first job offer wouldn't be a large school. It'll be a small college who knows where." Evan shifted in his chair to look at Eliana. "I'm not saying that there's no chance with her whatsoever, but it's definitely something for me to consider."

"It is." Eliana paused. She seemed to be fighting herself on whether or not to continue. "But that's a consideration with us, too, isn't it?"

His heart raced that she had mentioned 'us'. She'd been so careful in the past. "You have no roots. You travel a lot, but I feel like we could make it work one way or another. I think Paloma would hold it against me if I got offered a job in – say North Dakota - or someplace like that where she would be asked to go to a smaller zoo, or worse, where there was no zoo at all."

Eliana nodded. "It's something to consider with each of the girls. After all, asking Sarah to leave her family's orchard would be just as difficult."

It was certainly a complicated situation. Certainly this didn't seem like an ideal way to begin a relationship, and there were plenty of concerns to think about. Still, he was positive that God had led him here, so he would have to trust that He would work it out.

Eliana stood up to leave. "One more thing," Evan called out. She turned back around. "What does 'paloma' mean?"

A smile teased the corners of Eliana's mouth. "It means dove."

"Turtle dove." Evan shook his head. "Gotta admit you were creative."

Eliana flushed a little before she walked off. Evan watched her enjoying the way she spoke to the crew with respect, but authority. She had a great talent, and used it well. He frowned. Would they be able to make it work with her filming schedule taking her all over the world? If he ever did manage to move up from high school, he'd be traveling a lot, too, both for games, and recruiting. Maybe he should turn his focus more towards the rest of the girls rather than remaining fixated on Eliana. On paper, it just didn't seem to work.

Eliana motioned for him to join them signaling that Paloma was ready and filming for the second part of their date was ready to begin. He got up and went to the spot where Penny was motioning him to stand. Turning his attention from Eliana and possible issues with a relationship with her, he determined to give his full attention to Paloma and allow God to show him who should be his wife.

When Paloma came out, he drew in a deep breath. She wore a figure-hugging, bright red dress. Her hair was pulled back in a bun that gave the illusion of being careless, but he knew it had been carefully arranged. She wore stiletto heels that made her only about an inch shorter than him.

"You look amazing," he said with sincerity. Had he been looking at Eliana he would have seen her quickly look away, but his sole focus was on Paloma.

"You clean up pretty nicely yourself." She straightened his red tie that matched her dress perfectly. "Are you ready?"

He held out his arm, and escorted her to the car. Knowing from her application that she loved reptiles, and in particular turtles, Evan had been pleased to find that there was a gala at the aquarium to benefit the sea turtles.

Paloma's eyes were wide as she took in the sights at the gala. The aquarium itself was worth seeing with the myriad displays of ocean animals, but with it full of patrons dressed immaculately, an orchestra playing softly, waiters moving around with appetizers and drinks, and celebrities milling about, it was an impressive sight.

"I can't believe you would do this for me," she whispered.

"I had a feeling you would enjoy this. Having a good time, surrounded by amazing animals, and contributing to efforts that can rescue some of your favorites sounded like something that you would choose if you could."

Her eyes sparkled as she watched a sea turtle with a missing fin swim around the tank. "It's perfect." She leaned against his shoulder, and he wrapped an arm around her waist. Surprisingly, it felt natural.

They were called into the dining room where a five-star chef had prepared a meal for the event. Everything was delicious and beautifully displayed. They laughed, and talked through the meal, the crowds fading away as he focused on her alone.

It didn't feel like long before they were on their way back to the mansion in L.A. Evan was surprised at how much he had enjoyed his time with Paloma. Yet that one pesky question kept coming back: would she be willing to leave her home for him?

"Paloma, I have a question for you. I want you to really consider." He felt her watch him in the darkness of the car as he maneuvered through the interstate traffic. "You asked me if I would be willing to leave Iowa for one of you, now I'm asking you the same thing. If I were to be offered a job at a college somewhere, would you be willing to give up your dream job for me?"

The silence was overwhelming, but he stayed quiet giving her time to carefully consider his question.

"No," she said, softly. "I don't think I could do that." Tears shimmered in her eyes in the dim lights of the dashboard. "I can't imagine leaving my job for anything – or anyone. I'm sorry."

He smiled gently. "Thank you for being honest with me. I needed to know the answer."

When they arrived back at the mansion, he took her hands. "Thank you for an unforgettable evening." He kissed the back of her hands gently, and watched her walk away sure that she wasn't the one for him.

Paloma Valdez's post-date interview

"He was wonderful! I still can't believe that we spent the evening rubbing elbows with celebrities at an event to help sea turtles. It was a dream come true." She shrugged elegantly. "But I have a feeling that it will only be a beautiful memory, and nothing more. I hope that one of the other girls can offer him more than I can. He deserves it."

The 3rd Date

Pre-date interview with Lisette Blanchard

"If the way to a man's heart is through his stomach, then I have an advantage." Lisette's voice was laced with a French accent. Her hazel eyes framed with thick black eyelashes twinkled with humor. She tossed her bright red shoulder length hair. "The other girls may be prettier, smarter, funnier, but I can cook. And who could turn down a wife who can cook, eh?"

Eliana couldn't help but smile at Lisette's impish humor. Each of these women were so different from each other. Somewhere in the middle of Evan's date with Paloma, Eliana had decided to put aside her jealousy and enjoy the task in front of her. She determined to uphold the promise she had made herself at the dinner, to show each of these women in the best possible light, and in a way to cheer each one on.

As she had worked with the editor on the first date with Sarah, she had found herself feeling sorry for her. Her nerves were clearly evident, and it had made the date nearly a disaster. Together they had worked to highlight Sarah's friendliness, and bubbly personality. By the end, she was certain that Sarah would have plenty of viewers rooting for her to win Evan's heart.

Last night, it wasn't difficult to see the awe on Paloma's face as she watched the animals in the tanks, and that awe had spilled over when she had gazed at Evan as well. The natural affection between the two hadn't been easy to watch, but she knew it would be cheered on by those captured with Paloma's beauty and grace. Something must have happened in the car on the way home, though, because their parting had been more friendly than anything else.

Watching Lisette, Eliana knew that it would not be difficult to showcase her humor and fun. She was actually looking forward to watching her interact with Evan. Silently she thanked the Lord that she was starting to be able to distance herself from her emotions for Evan. Maybe by the time the show was over, she would even be pleased for whomever he chose.

******

For the first time, Evan wasn't told to wait in the foyer for his date to make a grand entrance down the staircase. Instead he was ushered towards the kitchen where he was asked to wait. He reviewed what he knew of Lisette from her file to figure out what might be about to occur.

Before he had too much time to think it through, Penny signaled for him to come in. He stepped into the kitchen to find Lisette wrapped in an apron, a large smile on her face. He couldn't help but smile in return.

"Surprise!" she called out enthusiastically. "We are going to cook together today." Her voice was melodic with her French accent.

"I'm not sure you want me underfoot," he protested

good-naturedly.

“Nonsense!” She hurried over, and before he could protest had an apron on him. “Anyone can cook. Haven’t you watched *Ratatouille*?” She laughed and he joined her. Lisette was going to be fun if nothing else.

“Yes, but I do simple cooking like grilling burgers or scrambled eggs. I’m sure you are capable of much more than I am.”

Lisette’s eyes twinkled. “Maybe a little bit more. I will be head chef, and you can be my sous chef. You may chop this onion for me to start.”

He was glad that his mom had insisted that he know how to do simple kitchen tasks like preparing vegetables so that he could do this on national television without looking like a complete idiot. In fact, he always cut the onions for his mom, because she couldn’t stand the chore and had passed it on to him.

“So I’m assuming you cook for a living?” he asked for the sake of the viewers at home.

Lisette straightened her shoulders proudly. “I own my café, Le Poulet Rouge.”

“What does that mean?”

“The red chicken,” she answered with a twinkle in her eyes.

“The red chicken?” He pointed to her hair. “Does the ‘rouge’ part have to do with your hair color?”

"Possibly," she chuckled. "I serve breakfast and lunch. My café is doing very well, too. My family was not very happy when I decided to move to the United States and open a restaurant. They thought it was foolish, but I have done well. My little café is often in the top ten lists for best breakfast and best café."

"You must be proud. How does your family feel now that you are successful?"

Lisette grew quiet even as her hands continued to prepare the food. After heaving a large sigh, she said, "They have not spoken to me since I left."

Evan looked at her with concern. He couldn't imagine the pain of not only being separated from your family, but having them so angry they refused to speak to you. "I'm so sorry, Lisette."

She shrugged and attempted a smile. "I have many friends who have become my family." She gestured towards the second floor where the women lived for the next few weeks. "And I am making more friends all the time, no?"

"Are you ladies becoming friends?" Evan hadn't thought about what it would be like to live with the competition. He would only see them all together twice throughout the show – once at the dinner to start the show, and once when he would reveal whom he had chosen.

"Oui. We talk about you, and how the dates have gone." She looked up at him with concern. "Poor Sarah did not think hers went so well."

Evan smiled at the memory. "Maybe it didn't start well, but it ended well. You can tell her that I only have pleasant memories."

Lisette's face brightened. "She will be so relieved." Deftly she tossed the ingredients in the pan.

"Is there a sense of competition between you all?" Evan's curiosity was piqued by her revelation that they were becoming friends.

"Perhaps some, but most of us only wish good for each other." She smiled at him. "We all want to win, but we don't want the others to fail." Frowning, she added, "Does that make sense?"

"I think so. You don't want to win because the others had bad dates, but because there's a genuine possibility of happiness together."

"Perfect!" Lisette beamed that he had understood. Turning around, she grabbed plates and began dishing up. He was impressed not only with the smells of the food, but how artistically she made it look. His stomach growled in response, and she giggled. "It's almost ready. Be patient."

"I'm trying, but it looks and smells amazing!"

Using a small table in a corner of the kitchen instead of the large formal dining room, they sat down after removing their aprons. They continued to chat, with Lisette often making Evan laugh out loud. Of the three dates he'd been on so far, Lisette was the most fun.

Before he knew it they were parting to prepare for their evening together. Evan turned to find Eliana waiting for him. It surprised him that he hadn't thought about her once during his time with Lisette. And yet, seeing her waiting for him made his heart race.

She smiled warmly. "That seemed to go well."

"French hen," he pointed out, nudging her side. "I'm actually having fun figuring out where they fit in the lyrics of the song now."

"Now that you trust me to not give you someone unsuitable merely to amuse myself?"

"You really did try to find girls that would fit well with me." He looked at her solemnly. "How did you know?"

Eliana shrugged. "I don't know. I just felt like these were the right girls." She perched on a stool at the island. "Any favorites of the three you've been with so far?"

Evan leaned on the counter next to her and thought it through. "Sarah did turn out to be endearing, but I'm not sure we 'clicked'. Paloma and I came to an understanding last night. She's beautiful and smart, but she's set where she's at." He smiled broadly. "Lisette has been a lot of fun, but so far she feels like someone who would be a good friend, but not necessarily someone I would want to be married to." He shrugged. "But we still have tonight, and I've learned that a lot can change after those evening dates."

Nodding, Eliana said, "I was thinking along those same lines." She looked up, and suddenly he was aware of how close they were to each other.

"You know I'm giving this my best shot, going into each date with my mind open, right?"

Eliana nodded, but seemed like maybe she had just realized how close they were to each other as well, and wasn't sure what to do about it.

A quick glance around the kitchen confirmed that they were on their own. "Good. So don't get mad at me for this." He pressed his lips to her cheek then trailed down to her lips. Pulling back, heart racing, he searched her face.

Her cheeks were flushed, and she seemed a little dazed. "No," she whispered. "I'm not mad." She stood up keeping her hands on the counter as if she was unsure her legs would support her. Clearing her throat, she added, "You should get ready for tonight." He watched her as she left.

Although he would give each date a fair chance, his heart knew who he would pick if he had the option to do so right now.

******

The arena had large banners advertising Cirque du Soleil. Lisette's eyes lit up as she saw them. "I've wanted to see this show, but they weren't coming anywhere near where I live."

"Are you really pleased? I was afraid maybe it was a stereotype or something to bring you to a French circus." Evan relaxed.

"No, no, no! I love Cirque du Soleil!" She slipped her arm through Evan's. "I'm so glad you thought of this."

To be honest, Evan had to thank his consultants. He had been hesitant, but they had persisted. Trusting their opinion, he had gone ahead with the plans. Eliana had chosen a wonderful couple to guide them in making the plans. They had told him that they had urged Sarah to not be quite so heavy-handed with the pears, but she had insisted. Other than that little issue, everything else had gone very well.

The show was entertaining although some of the contortions made him wince. Lisette was animated through the whole performance, cheering enthusiastically, gasping in pleasure, and gripping his arm tightly when one of the acrobats did a particularly intense move. It was almost more enjoyable watching her reaction than watching the show.

They were laughing when they entered the foyer of the mansion. "That was a lot of fun," Evan chuckled. "I really enjoyed my time with you."

Sobering, Lisette lowered her thick eyelashes. "As I did with you." She looked up at him expectantly.

He placed a hand on her cheek and lightly kissed her lips. Pulling back, he tried to conceal the disappointment that rushed through him. Kissing Eliana had been energizing, heart-pounding, and intense. Kissing Lisette had been – boring.

Something in her eyes told him that she felt it, too.

"Merci for a lovely evening." With that she walked away and Evan was left wishing that he had left it as it had been before the kiss. It had seemed to dampen both their spirits.

Lisette Blanchard's post-date interview

"Evan was so much fun! We laughed, and enjoyed our time together, but I think that maybe something is missing."

The 4th Date

Pre-date interview with Robyn Talbot

"I'm not a romantic. I watch these other girls swooning over Evan Garnett, and I think, 'That's not gonna be me!'" Robyn crossed her legs. She was curvy, and short, but had a strength and confidence about her that made her seem taller somehow. Her hair was cropped short in a no-nonsense manner that seemed to suit her professional attitude. Her dark skin was flawless, and her brown eyes revealed her intelligence. "I hope he's not looking for someone to fawn over him, because that's not gonna happen."

Eliana bit her lip at Robyn's words in amusement. Evan would surely be in for a completely different experience today. Yet, she really didn't think Evan wanted someone to be a doormat, that he would prefer someone who could intelligently discuss things with him. Perhaps Robyn would strike a chord with him. If nothing else, she would be unforgettable.

Eliana briefly touched her mouth. Speaking of unforgettable, she was having trouble pushing his kiss out of her mind. Then he had gone and kissed Lisette, too. At first she had been hurt, but then she had seen the flicker of disappointment in his eyes. She knew she shouldn't be rejoicing that it had been a flop, but she couldn't suppress the surge of happiness that flooded her.

She needed to push it all aside though. This competition was only starting. He was bound to kiss some of the other girls, and it was possible that one of them would feel a spark. To protect herself she had to put it behind her.

******

As soon as Robyn Talbot entered the foyer, Evan knew she was much different than the rest had been. Her personality seemed to fill the room. He couldn't help smiling at her as she shook his hand in a strong clasp.

"I remember you from the dinner," he mentioned.

"In a good way, I hope."

"You were the one who had doubts about this whole situation. You're a realist. I like that." He leaned closer. "I'd be lying if I said I didn't have doubts of my own."

"I'm relieved to hear that. I was afraid you were one of those mushy, romantic, girly men, and I can't tolerate that!" She started for the door. "Let's go."

He chuckled as he followed her. She certainly had a take-charge personality. In the car he found himself wondering where a down-to-earth person like Robyn would take him on a date. Her chatter was short and concise, her questions to-the-point.

"Be honest. Can you see yourself with someone like me?"

Evan looked over at her curiously. "You'll have to define what 'someone like me' means. If you're referring to your race, I believe that all members of the human race were created in the image of God. If you're referring to your strong personality, I'm enjoying it, and I think it could be an asset to have a strong wife with my football players hanging around the house. If referring to your looks, I think you're as beautiful as any of the other women in the house."

For a moment, Robyn seemed overcome. She smiled gently and seemed to drop some of her protective shield. "That answers my question." Glancing at him, she added, "You really think I'm beautiful?"

Evan smiled broadly. No wonder she had been so gruff. Most likely she had been comparing herself to all the girls in the mansion and thought she didn't have a chance, and so she decided to keep him at arm's length. "Absolutely! You have eyes that are a lovely brown, so dark they're almost black and they reveal your intelligence as well. Your face glows and your lips are full and beautiful." She smiled. "And that I think is your best feature! Your smile changes your face and makes you incredibly lovely."

If he didn't know better, he would think she was embarrassed. "So, you would give me a chance?"

"I am giving you a chance. I'm here, aren't I?"

"I mean, a real chance. Not just to please the producers because you have a woman of color to make you look good. Would you really, truly consider being with me?"

He watched her for a long moment, weighing her words carefully. "I already see so much in you that I like. I would be an idiot to dismiss you for some surface level reason." He paused before adding, "Can you do the same for me?"

She looked at him with smirk. "Now that I know you're not a girly-man I can."

Evan looked out the window as she pulled up in front of a large building. They climbed out of the car and stood side by side. "You brought me to a museum?"

"You're a history teacher, aren't you?" She looked up at him with her hands on her hips causing him to smile.

"Yes, I am. You're the first one who thought about doing something I might like instead of showing me things they like."

"Mm," she smirked, "that's good for me now, isn't it?"

Evan smiled broadly. "It's very good."

She took his hand and pulled him to follow her inside. "You can tell me all about the history of things if you want. I love learning new things."

They wandered inside and looked at the artifacts from tribes indigenous to California. "That's probably helped you be the success you are," he commented. "Being willing to learn is a valuable asset."

Smiling proudly, she said, "I'm the first in my family to go to college. I got my degree in business from UCLA, found an opportunity to open a business, and I haven't looked back."

"It seems like you're doing well with your company.

There's always a need for mobile phones in today's society." He knew from Robyn's dossier that she owned several mobile phone stores in the L.A. area.

"It's been good to me." She surprised him by downplaying her success. He had pegged her as a brash, proud woman, but he was getting the feeling that was all a façade to protect from those who might try to hurt her.

"Your family must be proud of you."

Robyn's face clouded. "I never knew my dad, and my mom left me with my grandma when I was four. Grandma got to see me graduate, but died of cancer a month later. She was very proud of me though."

"I'm so sorry."

Robyn shrugged. "You play the hand you're dealt is what Grandma would say. She said I could whine and complain about being dealt a bad hand, or I could play harder than anyone else and win. I chose to play hard." She lifted her chin, and Evan couldn't imagine anything standing in her way.

They walked into another section of the museum that was dedicated to the gold rush. "You know, I don't think you were dealt a bad hand. It was difficult sure, but if you had been given an easier life, I'm not sure you'd be as successful. It was fighting your way through everything that made you who you are."

Robyn smiled at him with a softness that surprised him. "You're the first person to tell me that. Thank you." Almost shyly, she slipped her hand in his. He was constantly being surprised by the layers in Robyn's personality. She was tough, but gentle, proud, and somehow humble, strong, and yet insecure. She was walking contradictions, and Evan thought that she would be an interesting woman to know better.

They walked through the museum hand in hand. Robyn asked intelligent questions proving that she really did love learning, and she eagerly soaked in his answers. At one point they passed a group of people who looked at them strangely (Evan assumed it was because of the cameras following them around), but Robyn simply lifted her chin and stepped even closer to his side.

When the group had passed, Evan leaned in close to her. "Do you feel out of place with me?"

She looked at him and bit her lip for a moment in indecision. "I feel out of place everywhere," she admitted.

"Do you think you would feel comfortable in a small town in Iowa?" He gave her a half-smile. "We don't even have one cell phone store."

They walked a little ways, and he could tell she was considering his question. "If I was there because of the man I loved, I could be comfortable, because the man I love would do anything he could to make it so."

He pulled her to a stop. "And would you do the same for the man you loved?"

Her dark eyes met his. "Absolutely! I think that's how I'll know when I'm truly in love – I'll want to protect him and be protected by him at the same time." She cocked her head to one side. “I know I can be domineering, I’ve pushed myself for so long I just naturally push others too. When I find the right man, I won’t want to dominate him. I’ll want to support him.”

Evan smiled and brought his hand up to her face. “That is wonderful.” Moving on in the museum he took her hand. “So how would you support a high school teacher/ football coach from a small Midwestern town?”

“Oh that’s easy. I would make all sorts of goodies for his team, and they would love to come to our house, but I would make sure they mind their manners. I’ll make sure he gets fed well and be available for him to talk to whenever he has a student he doesn’t know what to do with. And I’m sure I could find some sort of business to run in a small town.”

“I don’t picture you as the baking type somehow.”

“Don’t let my pretty face fool you. I make the world’s best brownies.”

Evan threw his head back and laughed. “I bet you do.” He looked over at her. “I also bet you would be a recruiting dream if that same coach moved to college football someday.”

“Oh honey, you know it!” Again Evan couldn’t help but laugh. The more time he spent with Robyn the easier she was to talk to. She had a thick shell, but when it cracked she was a sweetheart.

Evan had enjoyed the museum for its artifacts and history as well as the time he had with Robyn. He was eager to spend more time with her. The funny thing with her was that he could see falling for her, but he wasn't sure she could fall for him.

At the mansion, they parted ways, and he was glad to see that she had a big smile on her face as she went to get ready for their evening date. When they had started earlier that day, he hadn't known if she would have crossed him off by now or not.

"You won her over quickly," a voice said behind him mirroring his thoughts. He turned to find Eliana standing nearby.

"I don't think I've won her over. I've only given myself a chance to get through her shield." Evan looked at his toes for a minute. "Meet me tonight in the art studio?"

Eliana hesitated only a moment before nodding shortly. That was enough for him. He knew he was playing with fire, but Eliana was the closest he had to a friend in this crazy situation, and he desperately needed someone to talk to during it.

That night Evan took Robyn to a nice restaurant that had a jazz ensemble playing. She wore a bright blue one-shoulder dress and easily drew the attention of others although she never noticed. She closed her eyes and swayed in time to the music.

"My grandma used to play jazz music all the time, and I fell in love with it," she said. "It's probably not your favorite though."

Evan smiled. "I like some jazz – particularly older jazz.

It's not my favorite genre though."

"So you did this for me." She smiled at him with a softness he hadn't thought possible at the beginning of their date. "That was so sweet."

"You thought of me earlier today. It's only fair." He looked over at the musicians where a saxophonist was belting out a riff. "These guys are pretty good."

"They're improvising everything," she pointed out. "This isn't music that you've heard before or most likely will ever hear again."

"That takes some talent." He grinned. "My football team would fall apart if I said, 'Hey, go improvise something.'"

She chuckled. "My employees wouldn't fare much better." Her eyes rested on the jazz ensemble. "I always wondered if my daddy was musical or if mama enjoyed music. There are so many questions when you don't know your parents."

"I can imagine there would be. I guess I should appreciate how well I know my parents. It's something I take for granted."

Robyn's face grew determined. "That is one thing I want for my kids. I want them to know who their parents are and to be so incredibly loved that they'll never once doubt it."

"I have no doubt they will."

"I'm bringing things down, aren't I?" she asked with

a small smile. "You know what would cheer us up? Chocolate!"

Evan laughed. "That sounds like an excellent idea. Should we see what they have for dessert on the menu?"

Robyn shook her head. "I know this is technically your part of the date, but I know a place. Let's go." Evan gladly followed her out of the restaurant and was surprised when she started walking instead of going to the car. "It's close by," she said as if reading his mind.

Tucked away in an old strip mall was a small cupcake shop. From the outside it didn't look like much, but inside was bright and cheerful. A woman with gray hair and brown skin was behind the counter. Her face lit up when she saw Robyn. "My little birdie! Where have you been?"

"Here, there, and everywhere, Auntie June. This is Evan Garnett." Robyn's hand rested on Evan's arm in a proprietary manner.

"Mm, you got yourself a nice lookin' man, little bird! What can I do for you tonight?"

"We need something chocolate and delicious. So of course we had to come to you."

Evan enjoyed watching the banter between these two who obviously knew each other well.

"Now you're just flattering me," June responded before turning to Evan and adding in a low voice, "because it works." She gestured to a table. "Set yourselves down, and I'll be right back."

As they sat down, Robyn smiled at Evan. "I never choose what I'm going to have here, because Auntie June always thinks she knows best." She leaned over and whispered, "Because no matter what she brings it'll be wonderful!"

June came back in with two large cupcakes. She sat one in front of Robyn. "For you, my dark chocolate fudge cake with fudgy mocha frosting." Placing another in front of Evan, she continued, "And you seem like a young man who would enjoy a chocolate cake with a caramel core topped with dark chocolate fudge frosting and a caramel drizzle with a pinch of sea salt."

"These look amazing!" Evan said sincerely.

"Now Auntie June, those are the descriptions, but not the names of these cakes." Robyn's eyes twinkled. "What are they called?"

"Robyn's is the Up All Night cake, and Mr. Evan's is the Heart of Gold." June winked at Evan. "I think I picked the right ones."

Robyn shook her head. "She always has deep philosophy behind which cakes she picks." She picked hers up and took a bite. "Mm, and I don't even mind because it's so good. Try some." She reached across the table and gave Evan a bite of her cupcake.

"That is the moistest cupcake I've ever had!" Evan picked up his own eager to see how it compared. "Oh my goodness! This place is amazing!" He gave Robyn a bite of his, and although the caramel was messy, it was also the perfect amount of sweetness with the salt, and the bitterness of the dark chocolate frosting. "You picked the perfect place for us to finish."

As they left, Evan noticed several of the crew getting cupcakes from June as well. She even handed a box to Eliana who looked startled, but grateful as she accepted it. Evan had a feeling that June picked something special for each of them.

The mansion was, surprisingly, beginning to feel like home as he opened the front door and allowed Robyn to enter. She turned to face him, lips quivering slightly.

"Thank you for taking a chance on me. I think I close myself off too much, and you showed me that I can relax and be myself with men. Even if you don't choose me, I have hope that God will bring me someone who can love me for me."

"And I don't ever want you to settle for less," Evan added fervently. He pulled her close and kissed her lightly. There was warmth and affection, but nothing more.

One side of Robyn's mouth tilted as she looked at him after the kiss. "Oh, I won't settle for less. I hope you don't either. It'd be easy to do in this competition, settle for what's good enough, and miss what would be amazing. You deserve more than that."

Robyn Talbot's post-date interview

"I may be wrong, but even though Evan was a perfect gentleman, I think his heart already belongs to someone else. And whoever she is, she's a lucky girl."

******

Eliana could see Evan's figure as he paced the art studio. She clutched the box June had given her and stepped inside. "You wanted to see me?" Evan startled at the sound of her voice, but his face brightened just seeing her.

"I'm so glad you're here," he said fervently, leading her to the couch. "Not just here as in the art studio, but *here* going through all this with me. I think I'd go crazy if I didn't have someone to talk to."

"Well, talk away." She tucked her hair behind her ear. Every time she was with Evan it was a mixture of comfort and nerves. Such an odd mix. She often felt like she was on a first date, and at the same time like she was talking with her best friend.

"Which one did Auntie June give you?" Evan gestured at the box that Eliana had completely forgotten.

"Um, it's a s'mores cupcake." She opened it up to show him the chocolate cake with chocolate frosting, a large marshmallow that had been toasted, and sprinkled with graham cracker crumbs. "She called it Smokin' Hot."

Evan laughed, then gently touched her face. "She's right, you know."

Eliana blushed. "It looked like you had a nice day."

"I did. Robyn is going to be fantastic wife for some lucky man."

Eliana looked up shyly. “But not you?”

“Not me, and I think she knew it, too.” Evan turned to face her. “It took me a while to figure out how Robyn was the calling birds.”

“I thought that one would be easy.” Eliana chuckled.

“Well, the calling part I picked up on quickly, but it wasn’t until June called her little birdie that I figured out that she’s named after a bird.”

“You must have been dazzled by her to miss that.” Eliana nudged him as she took a bite of her cupcake. “Mm, you need to try this.”

“I shouldn’t,” he said with a hand over his stomach, but still he leaned forward and took a bite. “I have a feeling I should visit June every day while I’m here and try every single one of her cakes.”

“You’ll gain twenty pounds before you go home.”

“It would be worth it.” They both grew quiet for a moment, perhaps the thought of him going home reminded both of them that the end would come too soon, and they would be separated by more than distance. After he chose his bride at the end, they wouldn’t be able to have the same level of friendship that they enjoyed now.

“The first episode airs tomorrow,” Eliana mentioned, needing to break the silence. “I think it turned out well.”

“Does Sarah come across as likeable?”

Eliana loved him even more for his concern over

Sarah's appearance in the program. "I think she comes across as endearing and very relatable. I'm interested to know what your family and friends think after the episodes air."

"Actually, I am, too." Evan frowned. "Will I be able to talk to them about it?"

"You can talk about the ones that have aired, but not about the ones they haven't seen. Don't want any spoilers leaking out. And you can't let them know who you are going to pick or not pick." Evan nodded in understanding. "I should go. I still have some work to do tonight and it's getting late."

"Thanks for meeting with me. I enjoy our time together."

"Me, too." Eliana slipped out the door and whispered to herself, "More than I ought."

The 5th Date

Pre-date interview with Yi Wang

"I've heard nothing but good things from Evan's previous dates. I'm looking forward to spending time with him." Yi Wang had long, silky, black hair which she wore down framing her lovely face. Of Chinese-American ancestry, she had deep brown eyes, porcelain skin, and full lips. Soft-spoken and shy, Eliana knew it would be a different date than Evan's time with Robyn had been.

In seeming contradiction to her personality, Yi wore bright vibrant colors and chunky jewelry. She was one of the women that Eliana felt was a wild card in the competition. She wasn't going to be splashy, draw a lot of attention to herself, but her quiet, simplicity just might get Evan's attention.

"Nervous about tonight?" Penny asked Eliana as the interview finished. "Big premiere night!"

"I'm too busy to be nervous."

"But you are going to watch it, aren't you?" Penny followed Eliana around as she gave directions for Evan's interview.

"I've seen it already, remember? Several times actually."

"But it's different to see it at the end of the process,"

Penny protested.

Eliana whirled and faced her. “I know that, but I don’t have time to sit and watch it. I have to get the next episode ready and then the next. There’s no time to relax.” Truth be told, she’d watched the footage of Sarah and Evan so much, she thought she might go crazy if she watched it once more. She had to endure it while it happened and then pull it apart, put it together, and watch it over and over until it was perfect. It was bad enough watching Evan on his dates once, but she had to watch it repeatedly.

“Okay. I’m sorry I asked.” Penny put her hands up defensively, causing Eliana to sigh.

“I’m sorry, Penny. I’m stressed.”

“It’s all right.” Her twinkle came back as she admitted, “I’m looking forward to seeing the premiere tonight.”

“Enjoy it for both of us then.” With that Eliana went on to her next task. The sooner she could get all of this behind her, the better.

******

Evan wasn’t surprised when Yi took him to an art museum. She was a gifted artist herself, and had admitted on her application that her happiest moments happened when she was surrounded by art.

“I know you are an artist yourself,” Evan said looking at an abstract painting that made absolutely no sense to him. “What medium do you prefer?”

"Jewelry," Yi said softly. "I made all the pieces I'm wearing."

"They're beautiful. My mom would love the bracelet you're wearing."

Yi smiled proudly. "I've had some success with my venture."

"What pieces do you sell the most of?" Evan tilted his head as he came face to face with a sculpture of what appeared to be trash welded together.

"I've been doing well selling wedding rings."

Evan's eyebrows lifted as he turned his full attention to Yi. "Would these be golden rings?"

Yi looked surprised and a little confused. "Yes, I prefer gold even though it's not 'in style' at the moment. How did you know?"

Evan looked over at Eliana and grinned. "Lucky guess." They moved on and Evan was relieved that it was a landscape painting that he could admire openly. "So why gold?"

"In every culture gold symbolizes wealth and prosperity. I feel like as I make each piece I am wishing the couple success. I wish them to be prosperous in their finances, but more importantly, to have wealthy lives full of God, family, and love." Yi flushed slightly. "It probably sounds corny."

"It sounds very sweet," Evan assured her. They moved

in front of another painting that was merely a small blue square. "I have to ask, do you really consider this art?"

Yi giggled. "I suppose that's what makes art so wonderful. Everyone appreciates art in different ways. For some this might speak to them, and for others not so much."

"Be honest. Does this speak to you?"

Yi hesitated, trying to hide her smile. "Well, no. But I'll show you something that does." She led him to a Chinese scroll with a stone painted on it in ten different views. "This is a very old piece from the country my family came from. They moved here before I was born, but my parents have kept Chinese culture alive for me."

"At least this is something that I can tell what it is, and is something I wouldn't even attempt. Some of these I think my high schoolers could replicate with ease."

Yi giggled again. "You would prefer landscapes, portraits, things of that nature, I suppose."

"I like to look at it and say, 'I can tell what that is and it was done by someone who has more talent than a five year old.' I'm not picky."

At that Yi laughed loudly. She covered her mouth with her hand. "You are funny."

Evan had never thought of himself as funny, but it was nice to see Yi come out of herself a bit. He grabbed her hand. "For example, your bracelet is lovely, intricate, and I can tell it took skill and precision. I wouldn't trust a child to make me a replica for my mom."

Yi gave him a funny look. "You have mentioned your mom twice with this bracelet."

He dropped her hand. "I must be getting homesick after being away for so long." He moved on to a sculpture of a blue whale.

"My work is very personal. I design jewelry knowing that certain pieces will be worn by the person as an extension of their personality, not placed on a wall to fill empty space." She gestured to a canvas that seemed to be nothing more than white paint. "It tells me I've succeeded when a piece reminds a person of a loved one."

Evan enjoyed the art museum with Yi. He teased her about certain contemporary pieces, and she pointed out various artistic methods or gave information about the artists. He learned a lot from her, and enjoyed seeing her relax. Yet, he didn't feel as close to her as he had to some of the others.

That evening he took her to the art studio where an instructor was there to teach them to paint in watercolor. It felt strange to have the art studio full of crew, Yi, and the instructor – almost as if a private space had been invaded. He kept looking at Eliana to see if she felt it, too, but couldn't read her expression.

Yi took to the watercolor easily while Evan struggled. The instructor was patient, constantly assuring him that the beauty of watercolor was that it was easily fixed. By the end Yi had a lovely painting, and Evan had a picture that if he squinted his eyes kinda sorta looked like it was – something.

They wandered back to the mansion. Yi kept fiddling with her bracelet, keeping her head down. "I've been wondering how to do this," she finally said as they reached the doors. Still in the darkness, she slipped her bracelet off and handed it to him. "Your mom should have this." As he started to protest she put it in his hand and covered it with her own. "This was why I hesitated. I didn't want you to think of it as a bribe to pick me, or have you refuse because of how it looks. I told you that my jewelry is personal, and I liked it that it reminded you of your mom. Family is very important. Please give it to her, and tell her that I hope it will bring her much happiness whenever she wears it."

Evan smiled softly. "Thank you. I'm sure she will love it." He knew his mom would treasure the gift and would be quick to tell anyone about where it came from.

"Thank you for a fun day. It was so much more than I expected." Without waiting for him, she entered the house and left him standing in the dark.

Yi Wang's post-date interview

"Although Evan and I had a nice time, I could tell that it wasn't 'love at first sight' for either of us. I hope he remembers me fondly whenever he sees the bracelet."

******

Evan rushed back to the art studio, hoping to find Eliana there, but it was already deserted without a sign that anyone had been in there recently. His phone rang and he pulled it out, again hoping to see Eliana's number, but instead saw Kelly's. He had forgotten that the show was premiering that night.

Before he even had a chance to say hello Kelly squealed in his ear. "Oh my goodness! It was so exciting to see you on TV! You clean up nicely. And all the girls are going to love you – not just on the show either. Everywhere! Girls everywhere will love you!"

"Glad you enjoyed it," he murmured with humor.

"How is it going? Do you love it? Or do you hate it? You hate it, don't you?"

"It's been interesting, but you know my contract says that I can't discuss things with you."

Kelly sighed. "Oh I know. But Sarah was adorable. I love her!"

Evan chuckled. "I'm glad you do, but there are still many other women to see."

"So you like someone else better?" Kelly fished.

"I can't answer that, and you know it."

A voice in the background said, "Let me talk to him." Scott must have snatched the phone from his sister because he could hear her protesting. "Don't listen to Kelly. Sarah is fine, but there were some mighty attractive women at the dinner. I'd keep my options open."

"Give that back!" Kelly came back on the line. "Scott

thinks he knows everything."

Evan's interest was piqued. "What's Scott doing there?"

"Oh, he comes by all the time." Something in Kelly's voice alerted him to a change.

"Are you a couple now?" He couldn't believe that Scott had managed to change Kelly's mind since he'd been gone.

"No, not a couple," Kelly protested, but in the background he heard Scott disagree.

"If we're not a couple what are we?"

"Sounds like you guys need to figure a few things out." Evan was in disbelief. "What's going on?"

"It's just that Scott's been over a lot since you've been gone, and we've talked a lot."

"And she's falling in love with me!" Scott hollered.

When Kelly didn't immediately protest, Evan asked, "Are you?"

"He's not as annoying as I once thought he was," she replied. "I've found that I kind of enjoy spending time with him."

"That's kind of awesome. We could have a double wedding."

"No way! When I get married, all attention will be on me. And now that you're a super star, you'd hog all the attention."

The door of the art studio opened, and Eliana walked in. Evan was so glad that she stopped by, he couldn't prevent the smile that lit up his face.

"I've got to go, Kelly, but I'll talk to you later," he said, eager to talk to Eliana.

"I know you can't tell me what you think of the girls, but can I give you my opinion?"

"I think so. Although you have to know that I'm going to make my decision for me, not for you."

"Fair enough," she replied happily.

"And thanks for giving Scott a chance. He's a good guy."

"Yeah, he is. I'll talk to you later. I'm so proud of you." With that Kelly hung up.

Evan turned his full attention to Eliana. "Sorry. Kelly called. She liked the show."

"You didn't tell her anything about your dates, did you?" Eliana came nearer.

"No. I remembered about the clause in my contract. She however likes to tell me her opinion."

"As long as she doesn't influence you, I think that's okay." Sitting on a stool that had been occupied by Yi during the date, Eliana watched him. "What did she think of Sarah?"

Evan knew that she was concerned about the editing. Sarah in the full version of the date had not provided a very good view of herself. Eliana wanted the women to come across as loveable. "She loved Sarah. Thought she was adorable."

The relief was clearly evident in Eliana's posture as her shoulders relaxed. "That's great."

"My best friend, Scott, however would like me to hold out for some of the other women who he found more attractive from the dinner." He smiled at Eliana. "I think he half said it to irk my sister though. Annoying people is how he shows them he loves them."

"How do you show people you love them?" Eliana's eyes widened as she realized what she said. She leapt off the stool. "Sorry. Forget I asked that."

"Probably best if I could," Evan agreed. "I might do something that would make this even messier than it already is." He couldn't keep his mind from wandering to how good it felt to kiss her though, and his eyes wandered to her lips.

As if noticing his glance, Eliana licked her lips and took another step back. "I came in to tell you that the producers were thrilled with tonight's premiere. They think it will give the network a boost through the holiday season."

"That's great. Especially for you."

"Yeah." Her eyes fell to the floor. "Yeah, it's pretty great."

"Are you okay?" He took a step towards her which caused her to immediately take another step backwards.

"I'm fine. It's probably just the relief. You know when you've been building up for something and then when it happens there's kind of a letdown? That's all it is." Eliana backed away to the door. "I should let you get some rest. You were fantastic today – like every other day." Without another word, she disappeared into the darkness.

The 6th Date

Pre-date interview with Jillian Gosling

"I feel bad for Evan." The rest of the crew looked at Jillian in disbelief. Evan was living in a mansion filled with twelve beautiful women vying for his attention. How could she feel bad for him? "He's been running around on dates for the past five days, going here, going there. I think he could use a relaxing day. So that's what I'm going to do." She shrugged. "It might sound boring, but I'm guessing it will help him remember me at the end."

Jillian tossed her pale blonde hair over her shoulder. She had olive green eyes and freckles. Her features were dainty in keeping with her short stature and tiny build. Yet there was a strength about her as well.

As Eliana watched her on the monitor, it struck her that there was a certain similarity between Jillian and Sarah. Both had a cute, girl-next-door look to them rather than being a raving beauty, but where Sarah had been a bundle of nerves, Jillian was ready to take charge, and somehow still seemed laid back. Eliana didn't know how she managed it. When *she* took charge it was not in a relaxed manner. She wondered if Evan would notice the difference and then shook her head. It didn't matter. He wasn't here for her anyway.

When she had talked to Evan the night before in the art studio, he had seemed surprised that she wasn't over the moon about the good reception of the show. To be honest, she was a little shocked herself, but knowing that people were going to be rooting for certain girls, hoping that Evan would pick one of them, made her stomach clench uncomfortably. She blew out a breath. The sooner she could get the project done, the better for her sanity.

******

The pool shimmered in the weak December sunlight. Although it was too cool to be swimming, the pool was heated to a comfortable temperature. Evan placed his towel on a lounge chair and looked for Jillian. There was no sign of her, but he was certain she was near. Having been on several dates by now, he knew that once the cameras were set, Jillian would appear somewhere close by so that they could capture his first reaction at seeing her.

Vaguely he wondered if any of them had caught the way he looked at Eliana, and his reaction when she entered the room. Though he tried hard to hide it, there was no way that someone who was paying close attention would miss it. He knew his eyes lit up when she was near.

He needed to stop thinking about Eliana and focus on Jillian. They would begin shooting soon.

Almost as soon as the thought entered his mind, the call was given for places. He made sure he was where he was supposed to be, and soon shooting began. A tiny, blonde woman in a modest floral tankini came his direction. He put on a welcoming smile and moved to greet her.

"It's a little chilly for a swim. I'm glad the pool is heated," he said casually.

Jillian shrugged. "It's not terribly chilly. I'm from Wisconsin so this seems warm to me."

"Iowa winters are cold, but when I watch the weather I'm often thankful I'm not even further north," he commented.

"We're pretty tough," she boasted. "But I am pretty pale as well as tough. Could you help me with my sunscreen?" She handed him a bottle and turned her back to him. It was a good tactic. It forced him to touch her in a completely platonic and yet intimate way. He complied, but had to keep from glancing over to see how Eliana was reacting. He knew if some guy were rubbing sunscreen on her that he would be absolutely jealous. In a way, he hoped she was having a similar reaction.

When he finished, she turned and thanked him before adding, "Do you need me to get your shoulders?" She looked up at him adoringly.

"Um, thanks, but I'm wearing a swim shirt so I'm good." He was glad he had made that decision for many reasons. He didn't really like the idea of Jillian's hands on him when they had literally just met, but knowing that he would have been jealous with another man putting sun screen on Eliana, he didn't want to give her that possibility for jealousy.

"Oh, I understand." Jillian put on a bright smile to mask her disappointment. "So you ready to swim?"

"Sure, let's get going." Evan hadn't felt this awkward on the show since his first date. Jillian was trying a little too hard. He remembered how Sarah had been so uptight and nervous, and it had made her overly chatty. Perhaps Jillian was pushy because she was nervous as well. How could he put her at ease?

The water was a nice temperature as he dove in. "How about a few laps?" he suggested.

"Absolutely!" She took off quickly, and he soon discovered that she was adept in the water. Moving effortlessly, she easily beat him to the other end of the pool. Soon he was breathing heavy, but she seemed to be able to go all day.

He leaned on the edge of the pool panting. "You're a fast swimmer."

Treading water next to him, she smiled. "I'm around water a lot. I work at a wildlife sanctuary monitoring geese."

"What types of things do you monitor?"

"Migration patterns, health, mating rituals, and their offspring." Jillian looked at him coyly. "I'm especially interested in mating rituals."

He decided to let that slide. "So how many eggs do they typically lay?" Chuckling slightly, he murmured, "Six geese a-laying."

"Wait, what?" Jillian leaned forward. "Did you say something about geese laying?"

"Sorry, I guess it struck me as funny." When she looked at him strangely, he sobered. "But it's obviously not." He resisted the urge to look over at Eliana, but he heard a slightly strangled noise that made him think that she was smothering a laugh. "So anyway, geese's eggs?"

"On average they lay five eggs."

"That's very interesting." This time there was no denying the smothered laughter coming from where Eliana was sitting. Evan bit his lips to keep from joining her.

Angry now, Jillian climbed out of the pool and began to dry off. Evan followed not sure what he should do to diffuse the situation.

"What's the matter?" he asked. When she whirled on him with tears in her eyes, he took a step backwards. Obviously that was not the correct question.

"I thought you'd at least give me a shot. The other girls said you were sweet and a gentleman, but I seem to be the butt of some sort of inside joke. And I don't even know what I did wrong!" With that she burst into tears.

Feeling awful, Evan pulled her into his arms. "It's really nothing to do with you. The inside joke is about geese in general. I'm sorry that I hurt you."

Sniffling, she straightened and looked at him quizzically. "You have a joke about geese?"

He lifted a shoulder. "Sort of. It's a long story and not very interesting."

Jillian raised her chin. “Geese are actually quite majestic, you know.”

“Of course they are.” Evan tried to not remember the time a goose came after him at a pond when he was a child. The memory had made him skittish around all water fowl for years. “So, would you like to keep swimming?”

Jillian shivered under her towel. “Maybe the hot tub instead.” She smiled at him shyly.

Her forwardness at the beginning of the date had made him hesitant to get in the hot tub with her, but now she seemed more subdued and quiet. He decided he couldn’t afford to offend her any further. Gesturing for her to take the lead, he followed her to the hot tub. She sank into the bubbly water with a sigh.

“This is nice,” she said with her eyes closed.

He chose a spot near her, but not too close. He didn’t want to encourage physical contact if possible. “It does feel nice. I hadn’t realized how chilly I was until I got in.”

Evan leaned his head back and closed his eyes. Suddenly his eyes opened as he felt Jillian’s foot begin to caress his leg. He jerked away. “I’d better get ready for our date this evening,” he stammered as he left the Jacuzzi.

He wrapped his towel around himself and walked away before Jillian could scramble out. Even at a distance, he heard her ask innocently, “What did I do wrong?”

He was nearly to the door when he heard Eliana call his name. She caught up, breathless. “What happened in the hot tub? You were only in there for two seconds. Did she do something?"

Evan looked past Eliana, not wanting anyone else to hear. "She started running her foot up my leg. I don't know where she was going, but I didn't want to stick around to find out."

Eliana's eyes widened. "Wow. Forward, isn't she?" She glanced behind her then turned back to face him. "Thanks for telling me. I have to let her know, because she feels like you've singled her out to be the butt of the show. Plus she needs to know some boundaries."

Evan's shoulders slumped. "Maybe I should tell her."

"No," Eliana's lips tightened in determination. "I know the contract well. I can handle it. You go get ready, and I'll make sure that before this evening's date, Jillian understands what can and can't be done."

He watched as she marched back towards the pool. Not sure if he was more scared for Jillian or proud of Eliana for taking a stand for him, he prayed quickly for God to give her wisdom in handling the situation.

******

Jillian was lounging on a chair still in the pool area. Seeming relaxed, Eliana noticed that Jillian's eyes kept going to a group of her crew who happened to be some strong, good-looking men. No wonder she had opted to stay after Evan had left.

Eliana sat down on the chair next to Jillian. "We need

to talk."

Jillian sat up. "I hope you talked to Evan as well. It was humiliating the way he treated me."

Eliana stared at her feet, praying that God would direct her through this conversation, and keep her calm. "Do you remember what your contract said about physical contact?"

Jillian snorted. "Right, because we all read the contract word for word before we signed it."

"Well, it might have helped you understand this particular situation a little better." Eliana leaned forward. "See, Evan has some deeply held beliefs. We put a clause in everyone's contract that if there is unwanted physical contact they could be asked to leave, and their pay would stop at that time instead of continuing to the end of the show. This clause is in Evan's contract as well to protect you and the other girls. Your incident in the hot tub could be enough grounds to terminate your contract if Evan wanted or if I decided it went too far." Jillian's face whitened, but she said nothing. "Lucky for you, Evan is willing to give you another shot tonight, and I am willing to take you at your word that you were ignorant of the clause. I suggest you be a little more patient and not push forward with unwelcome contact."

Jillian looked away obviously uncomfortable. "I know I'm not as pretty as the other girls." She held out her arm and looked at it critically. "I'm so pasty I'm practically albino. I thought that I needed to do something else to make him interested in me."

"I picked you because not only did you have pretty, delicate features, but you were smart, passionate about your career, loved the outdoors, and were from the Midwest. Those are all things that I thought might be attractive to Evan, and I still believe they might be. You need to believe that it's enough as well." Eliana stood up. "Use other tactics tonight, because if your make him uncomfortable again, you're heading home."

Walking away she wondered how she was ever going to edit that disaster of a date to look like it was even semi-successful. She knew the producers would enjoy the drama and tension that it offered, but she was sticking to her promise to herself to portray each woman in the best possible light which meant she needed to try to salvage something from the date.

Her mind was still on that when they were setting up for the evening date. Apparently she wasn't the only one, because Penny caught up to her, and asked a very similar question. "How are you going to work the earlier date? Not only was it painful to watch, but it was short as well."

"I'm not sure," Eliana answered truthfully. "I just hope she's better behaved tonight so that I get some good footage here."

They set up on a pier as the sun started going down. Evan stood with fishing gear near the railing. At a distance, Eliana could still see that he was concerned. Knowing him, he was as concerned about how Jillian had felt after her reprimand as he was about a possible continuation of the afternoon.

Seeing Jillian was ready, Eliana set the action going. Jillian walked down the pier to Evan a tentative smile on her face. “Do you have a permit for those?” she teased, gesturing to the fishing poles.

“It’s all completely legal,” he answered. Eliana loved the ease with which he slipped into his role, and it was a role. Although he was himself, Evan had slowly developed a persona that he used with the women. He was charming, a complete gentleman, and caring – a man that was easy to fall in love with. Yet when he was alone with her, he was more relaxed, able to dive deep into any subject, funny, and affectionate. There was a difference. While Eliana knew that stage Evan would make women fall in love with him all over the nation, she loved the real Evan even more.

She sucked in her breath quietly. It’s not that she didn’t realize that she was falling for him before this point, but she hadn’t recognized how deeply her feelings went until that moment.

Pushing her roiling emotions aside, she focused in on the date between Evan and Jillian.

“I’ve never been ocean fishing,” Jillian was saying.

“To be honest, neither have I so we’ll learn together,” Evan answered. For a while they fished and shared past stories of fish they had caught or the ones that had gotten away.

After awhile, Eliana noticed a change in Jillian. Her cheeks were flushed with pleasure, eyes twinkling with humor, the tension gone. She looked pretty and fun. Eliana smiled and shook her head. Evan certainly brought out the best in each of the women. One thing she also noticed was that although Jillian was standing near Evan, she was keeping her hands to herself.

Both of them managed to catch a few fish that were able to be kept. Evan took her to a bonfire going on the beach. Without batting an eye Jillian joined him in gutting the fish. He complimented her on her efficiency, making her blush deeper. They fried the fish over the fire, and Evan pulled out a cooler with a salad, some fresh fruit and dessert in it.

After they finished eating, they leaned against the logs by the fire, and he put his arm around her. Slowly, she leaned her head on his shoulder. When he didn't pull away, a soft smile lit her face making her look lovelier than ever in the firelight. Eliana knew it was going to be a good shot, and tried to push aside the jealousy that always coursed through her when Evan touched someone else.

The stars and moon were out now, but there were still people on the beach milling around. Many stopped to watch when they saw the cameras. Eliana heard several of the women whispering when they saw Evan. When a few started to get phones out to take pictures and videos, security stepped in and blocked their view. As the crowd grew, Evan seemed to grow more uncomfortable, finally suggesting they return home.

Eliana had to admit she was relieved. Before the premiere had aired they hadn't caused a lot of disturbance. Now she was going to have to consider tighter security and cordoning off larger sections of public areas to avoid having to deal with fans.

Jillian's good night with Evan was little more than a handshake. Eliana knew Jillian was disappointed, but she felt like Evan couldn't trust her enough to do more.

Post date interview with Jillian Gosling

"I'll be absolutely shocked if he ends up choosing me, but I have no one to blame, but myself. I was too pushy, and I don't blame him." She shrugged. "It's a shame, because he's a really sweet guy."

******

Dude! Paloma is hot! Pick her! Evan smiled as he received Scott's text. It was immediately – and unsurprisingly – followed by a text from Kelly.

Do not pick her! She'll get in the way of your career.

Evan put his phone away. He wouldn't answer either of them. They couldn't know that he had already made up his mind. He just needed to work out the details.

The 7th Date

Pre-date interview with Kirstin Schwann

"Even if we don't hit it off, I'm looking forward to this date." Kirstin's feet bounced as she talked, a testament to her boundless energy. Her light brown hair had natural blonde highlights and her skin was tanned from being in the sun. Her muscular, athletic physique was apparent even in her casual clothing. "I planned something that I've wanted to do for a long time, but haven't had the chance to do. And I think he'll enjoy it as well."

Eliana sat back. Kirstin seemed the least concerned about whether or not Evan would like her. Was it an act or did she really not care? And if she didn't care, why had she applied to be on the show?

Kirstin had asked to meet Evan at the beach instead of in the foyer. When Eliana got there she realized why. Kirstin was at home outdoors. The sun shone off her dark blue eyes making them sparkle and bounced off her hair. Her tanned skin made her smile seem brighter. She was a bouncing, iridescent bubble in her element.

Evan couldn't stop his smile when he stepped onto the beach. Kirstin waved enthusiastically. "You look completely at home here," he pointed out.

"I am! I love being outside and at the beach is even better." Kirstin began walking through the sand. "I can't tell you how excited I am about this date. We're going snorkeling!"

"That sounds very cool. I've never been snorkeling before."

"Me either, but I've always wanted to go."

Evan looked out over the waves. "Do you enjoy the water?"

"I live in the water." She grinned up at him. "You're not the only high school coach. I coach a swim team at a high school in Arizona, and I'm also a gym teacher."

"That's fantastic. So if I get in trouble in the water, I at least know that you're a strong swimmer and can come to my rescue." Evan smiled at her, and Eliana could see Kirstin's shoulders relaxed. She cared more about this date than she had let on.

"I will definitely rescue you if you need it, but I doubt you'll need my help." Eliana gritted her teeth at their flirting, but forced herself to shake it off. She would have guessed that by date seven she would be used to it, but any date that was a success made her jealous, and any date that wasn't a success made her stressed about how she was going to fix it.

After the previous date's public interest, Eliana had received more security and permission to close off bigger areas for filming. They still garnered interest, but the people couldn't get as close to take pictures or videos on their phones. The fact that the studio was willing to spend more money to keep them safe and protect the secrets of the show told her that it was being received well.

An instructor met Kirstin and Evan at a boat dock where they got a quick tutorial on how to put on their wetsuits, how to use the snorkel, and what to do if they had trouble. He then took them out on the boat. Eliana and her crew followed in another boat. One cameraman was in the boat with Evan. As she watched them interact on the boat via monitors, Eliana noticed something interesting. Kirstin's eyes were as often on the instructor as they were on Evan. Her flirting seemed directed towards both men rather than one. Eliana raised her eyebrows as she watched, and wondered if Evan had picked up on it as well.

Not that she blamed Kirstin. She had no attachment to Evan, and the instructor was good-looking with dark skin and a muscular build from swimming. She was sure their love of the water was a bonding point as well.

It wasn't surprising that she felt the jealous feeling flit away, although she still chastised herself for feeling jealous at all. After all Evan wasn't hers and had never been intended for her. If Evan noticed Kirstin's divided attention, it didn't seem to bother him. He laughed and looked like he was enjoying the time out on the ocean.

There was plenty of laughter as they struggled to get into their wetsuits. "Oh this is becoming," Kirstin giggled after she got it on.

"I think you look fantastic," the instructor commented as he looked her over.

Evan only grinned. Kirstin didn't seem too upset by his

lack of response. After all, she had another man eager to dish out compliments.

Eliana followed their adventure on the monitor as the underwater camera linked to her computer. They appeared to enjoy their time, and underwater footage would be fun to edit. There had been plenty of sea life for them to see, and when they climbed back onto the boat they were eagerly discussing everything they had seen. It had been a successful date, and one that Eliana wouldn't need to improve at all. A welcome relief after his date with Jillian.

Before long they were heading back to land, and Kirstin's flirting with the instructor became more pronounced. It was he who helped her out of the boat as Evan watched with amusement. As they prepared to leave, the instructor managed to slip Kirstin a business card with his personal cell number on it. While Evan at first seemed not to notice, a wink in her direction let her know that he had seen it all.

"I know you love the beach, but I have to get some things ready for our date tonight," Evan said. "Why don't you stay and enjoy yourself, and I'll see you later tonight?"

Eliana smothered a smile at how easily Evan had managed to leave Kirstin with her admirer without any awkwardness. Kirstin eagerly took him up on the offer and agreed to meet him in the foyer that evening. Eliana shook her head as she trudged through the sand back to the vehicles.

"Hey!" Evan rushed to catch up to her. "Can I ride with

you?" He grinned at her. "It'd be nice to compare notes."

"I think that's an excellent idea." Her pulse raced at the chance to be alone with Evan.

After they got on the road, Evan started laughing. "I think I've lost one of the girls before I even really tried to win her."

"It appears that way." Eliana glanced over at him. "You don't seem broken up about it."

Lifting a shoulder, Evan replied, "Kirstin is cute, but not for me." He looked over at her with an intensity that made her blush. He grinned at her discomfiture. "But I have to take her on one more date."

"Yes, you do." Eliana shifted in the car seat. "At least this episode will be easier than the last one was."

"Are you going to include Romeo in it?" he asked with a smirk. "A love triangle always draws attention."

"I'm not sure how I'll put him in it, but he'll have to be part of it. I don't want Kirstin's interest to distract from you though."

"I'm fine with it."

Eliana giggled. "I know you are, but I'm thinking about the viewers and producers."

They pulled into the driveway, but stayed in the car, both unwilling to end their alone time together. "Does it bother you at all? Seeing me with all these girls?"

"Yeah, it does," Eliana replied honestly, "but I have to push it aside."

"I would be completely jealous if the roles were reversed," he admitted as he turned in his seat to face her. "I'd be tempted to make each one look bad so no one liked any of them."

Eliana sighed. "I can't do that. And honestly, I like most of these girls. Jillian was a little rough, but most of them are very sweet. I don't want to vilify them."

"And I think I love you even more for it."

The silence was thick in the car as both of them absorbed the words he had spoken. "You love me?" Eliana whispered.

"I thought that was pretty obvious." He raised his hand and caressed her cheek.

She swallowed hard. "You can't love me."

Half of his mouth turned up. "Yet I do." He pulled away, leaning against the car door. "I know I have to finish the show, and I will keep giving each of these dates a fair chance, but I know who I would choose if I had the opportunity."

Eliana's breath caught in her throat. "Me?"

He laughed deeply and he leaned forward and kissed her mouth softly. "Always you."

She closed her eyes and leaned her head against his. Her mind whirled with various emotions, most too difficult to pin down or name. "We should go in before someone sees us."

He sighed, but pulled back. They climbed out of the car, but before they reached the door he spoke. "One last thing before we go in." She turned to face him. "What is the seventh day?"

Eliana smiled. "Seven swans a-swimming."

"Kirstin Schwann the swim coach. Clever." He leaned in close and whispered. "Your cleverness is just one of the many things I love about you. Remember that."

******

Evan tried to keep his mind on Kirstin, but kept going back to his time with Eliana that afternoon. That time, short as it was, had felt more like a date to him than any other date he had been on.

The seafood restaurant he had chosen for their evening date was beautiful. They sat on a deck that faced the ocean, a fire pit nearby keeping them warm from the cool air. The food was amazing with fresh ingredients prepared in a way that highlighted the delicate flavors of the fish.

Kirstin had dressed in a deep blue, long sleeved dress that clung to her figure. Her hair had been curled and styled, and she looked beautiful. In spite of that, he found his gaze wanting to wander over to Eliana who had on jeans and a sweater with her long dark hair in a simple ponytail.

His date didn't seem to notice. In fact, she seemed

distracted as well, and he assumed that she was wishing she could be with the snorkeling instructor instead of him. The conversation was stilted and awkward as neither of them wanted to be there.

After a prolonged stretch of silence, Eliana called for the filming to stop. Marching over, she leaned against their table and kept her voice low. "I know you don't want to be here, and would rather be with your new friend from this afternoon," she directed at Kirstin, "but you're killing me. This is supremely boring. Please think of each other as old friends catching up instead of being on a date. Anything to get the conversation going. I don't want to have to script this."

Kirstin blushed and looked embarrassed. "I'm so sorry." She looked over at Evan. "I really didn't mean for anything to happen."

He put his hand up. "It's really okay. I don't expect every woman to fall at my feet."

Kirstin looked relieved. Turning back to Eliana, she added, "I'll be better. I promise."

"Thank you." Eliana went back to her spot and called for action to resume.

"When you teach gym do you have outdoor classes or indoors?" Evan asked, trying to get some conversation going for Eliana's sake.

"I usually do outdoor sports by my own choice. And fortunately in Arizona I have the ability to be outside most days of the year. I do tennis and softball most of the time, but I'm happiest at the pool." Kirstin brightened up and began telling him stories about her students, the championships they had won, and the excitement of seeing a swimmer achieve something they hadn't thought was possible.

Evan contributed with his own experiences with his football team, his history class, and the dreams he had for their future. He could see Eliana settle back into her chair out of the corner of his eye and knew that they were doing better.

Over coffee and dessert, Kirstin admitted to him, "My sister entered me into this show. I wouldn't have done something like this on my own. In fact, I was shocked that I was chosen. If I had known I would be, I wouldn't have let her submit my application." She smiled up at him. "But I'm glad now that I did."

The viewers would assume it was because she had met him, but he knew that if she hadn't been on the show she wouldn't have met her Romeo while they snorkeled. "My sister submitted an application for me as well, and I was not expecting to be chosen either. But like you, I'm glad I did, too. I would have missed out on so much." It took everything in him not to look at Eliana, but he was certain that she knew what he meant.

When they got back to the mansion, Evan felt relief in knowing that it would be a platonic good-bye. Neither of them was interested in the other, and both had feelings for someone else. He held out his hand, and kissed her on the cheek. "Good luck to you and your swimming team."

"Same to you. I hope your team does well next year." Without another word, she walked away.

Evan slipped away as the crew tore down the equipment. Going up to his own wing, he collapsed on the bed. It was kind of surprising that this large space felt like home. Actually as he thought about it, it wasn't the mansion that felt like home, but his suite. It was his space, separate from the busyness and drama of the show.

With that thought, his phone vibrated letting him know he had a text message.

Have Lisette make me something! That looked delicious, Scott wrote.

You need more than food. I still like Sarah, but Lisette would be okay, too. Who are you leaning towards? Kelly added.

Evan sat up to type. *You know I can't tell you that.*

Ah! I want to know!

Evan chuckled and put his phone away. Kelly would just have to wait like everyone else.

Kirstin Schwann's post date interview

"While I had a nice time, I think both Evan and I discovered that there was no spark. It was more like talking with a co-worker than a boyfriend." She smiled softly. "And I think there's someone better out there for both of us."

The 8th Date

Pre-date interview with Marian Merkel

"I was afraid that being in the second half of the group of girls that by this point Evan would have already found the girl of his dreams, but none of the others seem sure they've got it clinched. So I have hope that he'll at least have an open mind on our date." Marian's gray eyes were serious, lines next to her mouth indicating some tension, maybe some nerves. Her strawberry blonde hair hung in tight ringlets around her face softening the strain on her face. "I've heard he's very nice, but I'm hoping that maybe I'll be 'the one'." She shrugged almost embarrassedly.

Eliana ducked her head. Maybe she should have done this all differently – kept her distance from Evan or chosen a different guy when she realized they were falling for each other. It wasn't really fair to Evan or these women that he'd already given his heart to her. While a part of her rejoiced in that, another part of her wished it was different so that these women had a shot at Evan.

As Marian shook her curls, Eliana took a breath. The reality was that they did potentially have a shot at Evan. He had told her that he was trying to be fair with each of them, and there was a chance that one of them might sweep him off his feet. Was she prepared to deal with that if it happened?

******

Evan paced the foyer. He was trying to keep his focus on the show, but all he wanted was Eliana. How was he going to finish the show fairly when it was becoming more and more difficult to ignore his feelings for Eliana?

Lord, help me. I love Eliana, but to help her I need to give these other women an honest chance. What if my feelings for Eliana are only a shadow of a greater love you have for me, but I'm pushing that girl away? Am I overthinking this? He ran his fingers through his hair in frustration.

"Just don't overthink it, okay?" A voice brought his attention back to the present. He looked over to find a member of the crew talking to him.

"I'm sorry. What did you say?"

The guy smiled and shook his head. "Man, I knew you were distracted. Just don't overthink it, and you'll be fine. Act naturally."

Evan nodded. "Yeah, I can do that."

The man thumped him on the back. "I know you can."

Evan looked up at the ceiling for a moment. Was that God's answer or was he reading into things? He shook himself. Don't overthink. Act natural. Get through the next few dates. Simple enough.

A cute, strawberry blonde came in, a tentative smile on her face. "It's so nice to meet you – again. I guess we met at the dinner. But in case you forgot I'm Marian Merkel." She put a hand to her face. "And I'm chattering like an idiot."

"It's nice to meet you, Marian. What are the plans for this afternoon?"

"I love movies, but I've never been to Hollywood. I thought maybe we could go there? Is that okay?"

Evan smiled and put a hand on her shoulder. "It's a great idea. Don't be so nervous. I promise not to bite."

Marian smiled shyly. When they got in the car, she admitted how nervous she was. "No one seems to have sparked any interest in you yet, and while I thought that should make me more relaxed, instead it's making me more nervous. I feel like I need to really, really impress you."

Evan thought for a moment over what she had said. "Remember that this goes two ways. There may be a spark on my side, but if there's none on yours then we need to know that, too. Relax and be yourself. I want to know you." And it was true. He did want to know her, and he really didn't want her to be so tense.

She sighed. "I'm not really worth knowing. There's nothing special about me."

"Of course there is. You are a unique creation of God's, a masterpiece that He is adding to daily. Don't let anyone make you feel like you're unimportant."

Marian looked over at him in wonder. "You really

believe that?"

"Absolutely! We might be a little rough around the edges, but God makes beautiful things." He glanced over at her. "And you are no exception." She smiled slightly and looked away. "So, tell me about yourself. Besides being a movie buff, what else should I know about you?"

"I own a couple of dairy cows and make artisan cheeses that I sell at farmers markets." She shrugged. "It's not very interesting."

"What's your favorite cheese to make?"

"Cheddar and mozzarella are my biggest sellers, but I enjoy manchego the most. Traditionally it's made with sheep's milk, but I've made it with cow's milk and it's delicious."

"I'm not sure I've ever tried that kind." Evan found a parking spot and pulled in.

"I'll have to send you some." She blushed prettily.

"I'd like that." Evan went around and opened her door. They toured the walk of fame, found their favorite actors footprints, and saw Grauman's Chinese Theater before going out and taking a selfie in front of the Hollywood sign. Evan made sure to take lots of pictures, playing tourist, so that regardless of what happened between him and Marian, she would always have photos to remind her of their day together. As the day progressed, she loosened up, seeming to enjoy their time together. And he was surprised to find that he enjoyed the time, too. During the afternoon, he hadn't thought about Eliana once even though she was nearby the whole time.

Back at the mansion, Marian turned to him. “This has been the best afternoon ever. Thank you.”

“It was your idea. Wait to thank me tonight. You may not like my idea so well.”

“I think I’d like to do just about anything with you,” she admitted shyly. Impulsively, she stood on tiptoes and kissed his cheek before dashing away.

“You’ve won her over.” Evan turned to find Eliana behind him. “Very different from yesterday where at this point you’d already lost Kirstin.”

He nodded. “I hope I’m not leading her on.”

“All of them know they are one of twelve options, and you are just as likely to pick another person as you are them.” She shrugged. “I think they’re all being cautious with their hearts.”

“I guess I have an advantage in that then. There’s only one of me.” Evan faced her. “Are you okay?”

“With Marian falling for you? Professionally, yes. It makes a wonderful episode. Personally,” she heaved a deep sigh, “I’ll survive whatever the outcome is. Don’t let me come between you and whoever you fall for. I want the best for you – even if it’s not me.” She touched his arm. “Just don’t overthink it. God will direct.”

He smirked. “That’s been the theme of the day.”

“Must be what you need to hear. It’s okay to fall for

someone else." He could see the strain in her eyes even though she tried to appear relaxed. "I'd rather you pick someone else now than choose me and wonder if it would have been better with one of them." She gestured towards the stairs.

"You're right, of course." Evan shoved his hands in his pockets. "Eight maids a-milking."

Eliana's lips twitched. "Maid Marian the dairy farmer."

Evan burst out laughing. "I hadn't figured out the name part yet. How am I going to spend the evening with her without thinking of that?"

Eliana sobered. "You have to. She'll be crushed if you don't take her seriously. Of all the girls so far, she's the one who has taken the risk of kissing you first, and she's not a brash lady."

Eliana's words rang in his mind as he waited for Marian that evening. He had to be tender with her. She had shown that she was more fragile than the others, and yet she had been the most willing to take a chance on him.

A stir made him look up. She came down the stairs in a floor length sea foam green dress with sparkles shimmering in the full skirt. Her hair was perfectly framing her face which had a delicate make-up palate. A beautiful diamond necklace encircled her neck with matching bracelets on her arm. She looked like an angel.

Dressed in the tux Eliana had insisted he had needed, Evan met her at the foot of the stairs. "You look absolutely beautiful."

She blushed and took his arm. He led her to the waiting limo outside. Eliana hadn't surfaced yet, but he knew she would follow them.

"So where are we going tonight?" Marian asked. "I was only told to dress formally."

"There's a movie premiere tonight done by the same studio that is producing our show. So we got an invitation to go." It was good publicity for the show to have them on the red carpet. Now that the show was airing they would get a warm reception from the media as well as the fans.

Marian paled. "We're going to walk the red carpet?"

"We are." He put his arm around her and pulled her close. "I hope you've practiced your red carpet smile."

She giggled. "Like every day of my life," she admitted. "This is a dream come true."

They pulled up to the theater, and Evan exited first before turning to help Marian out of the limo. Immediately camera flashes went off and people called out to them. They proceeded down the carpet, pausing at certain places to pose for pictures or to do an interview.

A TV personality put a microphone in his face. "How does it feel having twelve beautiful women fawning over you?"

"They've been fantastic. Each has been charming, and no matter the outcome, I know I've met some lifelong friends through this experience," Evan replied.

"And which date is this?" she asked next.

"This is my eighth date, Marian Merkel, who is a wonderful artisan cheese maker as well as a movie fan, and the sweetest date I've had so far. She's a masterpiece."

Marian flushed, but kept smiling brightly even as the reporter turned her attention to her. "How has it been sharing the nation's most eligible bachelor?"

"There's actually been a surprising amount of camaraderie between us. It's not that we don't each want to win, but we're together so often – more than we're with him to be honest – that we've become friends." Evan was proud of the poise that Marian demonstrated.

"If it can't be you, which one of your competitors would you want to win?"

"Robyn Talbot," Marian answered immediately. "She would be such a good match for Evan, and she truly cares about him."

Evan tried to mask his surprise. He had felt strongly towards Robyn as well, but he hadn't realized that the others talked about things so openly.

With the interview completed, they moved further down the red carpet. "You were wonderful," he praised her. "Your answers were thoughtful and you were so poised."

"My heart is pounding," she laughed. "I still can't believe I'm here."

He smiled at her, but then his attention was caught by something else. Eliana stepped out of a limo wearing a deep red one-shouldered dress that clung to her figure before falling in folds at her feet. Her long dark hair was pulled back in a loose side bun, and her make-up was more elegant and exotic than he'd ever seen. He sucked in his breath as he watched her walk the carpet with confidence, chatting easily with reporters and actors, a bright smile on her face. While Marian was a dainty beauty, Eliana was absolutely gorgeous.

He forced himself to force his attention back to Marian, hoping she hadn't noticed his distraction or what had caused it. Fortunately, Marian seemed oblivious to his lapse as she chatted eagerly about the movie they were about to see, and barely contained her excitement over all the celebrities around them.

When the movie ended, Evan couldn't have said what it was about, but Marian gushed over it. He caught a glimpse of Eliana and placed his hand on his chin. She immediately scratched by her ear before disappearing into the crowd.

While he was quiet all the way home, Marian kept up her excited chatter about the night until they were in the foyer. She sighed ecstatically. "That was the best night ever. You were right to have me wait to thank you until now." She came over and pressed her lips to his. "Thank you." The sparkle in her eyes and faint smile on her face told him that she felt more from the kiss than he did, or maybe it was still reaction from the excitement of the evening. He stepped back.

“I’m glad you enjoyed it.” She smiled before ascending the stairs.

Evan hurried to the art studio. Pacing in the darkened space he relived the moment he saw Eliana coming out of the limo. She had been so beautiful and had seemed almost unattainable.

The door softly opened. He hurried over and pulled her into his arms. “You looked absolutely beautiful tonight.” He kissed her with more passion than he had allowed himself before. “I needed to see you.”

Eliana sighed in his arms. “Just another part of my job.”

He held her tightly. “I think I’ve had my answer,” he said softly.

He felt her shake her head. “You still have four more dates. You can’t be sure yet.”

Sighing he released her. “I suppose you’re right, but I wish I could end it right now.”

“What if one of the last four is more than you’ve ever imagined?”

“You’re more than I imagined,” he replied, reaching out to gently touch her shoulder.

“Give them a chance.” Eliana sighed deeply. “I think I’ve been working too hard. I feel so tired tonight.”

He kissed her head lightly. “Get some rest. I’ll see you tomorrow.”

She waved slightly as she left the art studio. Immediately, his phone buzzed.

I changed my mind. Robyn is my new favorite. Can you imagine recruiting with her as your wife? Evan chuckled at Scott's text. He was certain that he was right. Recruits would come just for her.

For once, Scott is right. Robyn is amazing! Evan raised his eyebrows. He couldn't remember the last time that Scott and Kelly agreed on anything.

Marian Merkel's post date interview

"It was a fairy tale! I felt like a princess out with prince charming. It was everything I had dreamed it would be. I can't imagine anything that would have made it better. A perfect evening with the perfect man."

The 9th Date

Pre-date interview with Clara Parker

"I'm interested to see Evan outside his comfort zone a little bit. You can tell a lot about a person when you push them and watch how they react." Clara's green eyes sparkled at the thought of pushing Evan a little bit. She was tall and slender. Her skin was the color of a latte and her hair was full with tight curls. Her face was exotic, sophisticated, and impish all at the same time giving her the feeling of being someone who could be your best friend if only you could get near enough to know her.

Eliana rubbed her forehead as the interview concluded. "Are you okay?" Penny asked from behind her.

"I think I should take a sick day. Do you think you could cover for me today?"

Penny's eyes widened comically. "Me? I don't know. I mean, it's going so well, but what if I mess it up. I'm not you. I don't have the experience."

"The crew knows how I like it set up. Your job is easy right now. Basically just let the dates happen and make sure you don't miss anything interesting." Eliana sighed as she began to sweat. She was definitely sick. "I really need you to do this for me."

Penny's look changed from fear to concern. "You really

don't look well." She took a deep breath. "I'll manage. You go get some rest."

Eliana smiled briefly before calling over a few key members of the crew to explain the change. They all assured her that they would take care of it and urged her to go back to her cottage and rest. Now feeling exhausted and chilled, she couldn't help, but agree with them.

Back in her cottage she got back in pajamas, put her hair up in a sloppy braid, and immediately went to bed wrapping herself in the warmest blankets she had. Before falling asleep she prayed that her illness would be of short duration, and that the show would run smoothly without her. A tiny voice hinted that it might be for the best. Without her there, Evan wouldn't have his attention divided and could give Clara all his focus.

******

Evan sensed a shift in the mood of the crew as soon as he entered the room. There was more chatter, less focus. His eyes wandered the room until he found Penny. "What's going on?" he asked.

Penny looked up at him frazzled. "She's sick – like she really did not look well at all. So it's all on me today." She giggled nervously before grabbing his forearm in a death grip. "Please make this easy on me."

"I'll do my best." When she released his arm, he rubbed it with his other hand. "Is Eliana going to be okay?"

"I think she has the flu or something." Penny's eyes widened. "Don't you go and get sick! You're even more important that she is!"

Evan briefly thought about their kisses the night before. He hoped he didn't get sick, too, but it was possible that he would catch it from those moments. "Maybe getting some hand sanitizer and vitamin C would help," he suggested.

"Good idea." Penny rushed off and he assumed she would be sending out a runner to go get the items.

His thoughts were fully set on Eliana in her cottage. He wanted to go to her and see that she was okay, wanted to get whatever she might need, wanted to take care of her, but that couldn't happen. He nearly missed the call to action because of his distraction.

Clara Parker entered the room with an elegance and grace that no one else had possessed. Even in workout clothes she looked sophisticated. Evan briefly wondered what she had in mind for him. She had requested that he be ready for a workout so he figured they were going to be active. Probably a good thing since it would help keep his mind on Clara and off of Eliana.

"Are you ready to leave your comfort zone?" Clara asked with a smile.

"I guess we'll have to see," Evan admitted. "I hope I'm up for any challenge."

When they pulled up in front of a dance studio, Evan wondered if he'd been too quick in his response. Clara laughed at his expression. "It won't be as bad as you think."

"Sure, easy for you to say. You studied ballet at Julliard and are a principle ballerina in New York."

Clara glowed for a moment revealing how proud she was of her accomplishments. "True, but we all start somewhere." She led him inside where a middle aged woman met them, introducing herself as Madame Smirnov. She had a thick Russian accent and barked at them like a drill sergeant. "Madame Smirnov is one of the finest ballet teachers in the world," Clara told him under her breath.

"I'm sure she's one of the toughest," Evan responded.

She led them through a warm up with stretches that he could never hope to do before teaching him the basic positions of ballet. Clara easily did the routines that he was certain were intended for preschoolers, and made them look easy and beautiful.

Moving to the barre, he was put through more agonizing exercises. Clara chuckled as she watched him. "I thought ballet was supposed to help football players."

"It might, but I'm a coach, not a player," he grunted.

Clara threw her head back and laughed. "You're a good sport at least. You haven't complained at all."

"Oh I've been complaining. It's just been in my head." Again she laughed, and he smiled in return.

Just when he was wondering how much more he could take, Madame Smirnov called enough. With condescension she told him that he had performed adequately before she left the studio with her back straight and chin up. Evan collapsed on the wood floor while Clara did an intricate pattern of twirls and leaps. He watched her, admiring how simple it looked when she did it and how graceful she was.

"When did you start ballet?" he asked.

"When I was three. My mother worked three jobs to help me be able to afford to go, and even at that young age I was aware that it was a sacrifice for my family. I worked harder than anyone else because of that. When I was thirteen I got the lead part of Clara in *The Nutcracker* in a local production company and I loved it."

"Were you named after the main character in *The Nutcracker*?"

Clara took a seat next to him on the floor only slightly winded. "No, I was named after my dad's grandmother."

"I'm sure you've made her proud."

Clara smiled sadly. "I never met her. She passed away before I was born which was why I was named after her."

"Well, I'm certain the rest of your family is very proud of you."

"My mama is over the moon about my accomplishments. I've tried to thank her for all she sacrificed with gifts, but she says that watching me dance is all the thanks she needs." Clara smiled softly.

"What about your dad? Siblings? Grandparents?"

Clara sighed. "My daddy was killed in a car accident when I was only one. My older sister and I are not very close. She always felt that I didn't deserve the sacrifices my mother made for my dance classes – or maybe was jealous of them. And my grandparents have all passed away by now as well, although my dad's parents did get to see me as Clara."

"You've had a difficult life," Evan pointed out.

Clara shrugged. "It made me stronger."

The door to the studio opened and a Latino man entered. He immediately told them to get up, and then started instructing them on how to waltz, tango, and foxtrot. Clara's training and grace made it easy for her to learn the new steps, but Evan was constantly fumbling for the right move causing them to both break down with laughter.

By the end, they had a dance choreographed that they performed together, and he was even able to do it without mistakes. Evan distinctly heard Penny sigh after the dance was finished, and it made him wonder how Eliana would have felt watching him dance with Clara. He wondered how she was feeling, and he had to pull his attention back to the date with Clara.

"Thank you for pushing me out of my comfort zone. It was a lot of fun."

"I'm glad you were such a good sport about it. You're not half bad."

"I'm not half good either," he added which made her

start laughing all over again.

That night he took her to a performance of *The Nutcracker* done by a youth ballet company. All the dancers were under eighteen and while it lacked the polish and sophistication of a professional dance company, it was delightful to watch the children dance with large smiles on their faces.

Throughout the performance Clara held his hand, her own smile rivaling that of the proud parents. During intermission, she laid her head on his shoulder. "Sometimes it's good to remind yourself of what it was like to be a child. Often dance is simply work for me now. I miss the childish joy that came with putting on a pretty costume and dancing on the stage for my mom. It was as if she was the only one in the audience for me."

"They're cute to watch, too," Evan replied. "I loved that one little girl who kept waving to her family throughout her whole dance."

Clara sighed. "Oh to be a child again!" She was quiet for a moment then shifted her head so she could see his face. "Do you want children?"

Evan raised his eyebrows. "Someday I would. Why do you ask?"

She raised her head from his shoulder and shifted to look at him. "Having children in my profession isn't exactly easy. I've thought about it a lot since I made ballet my career. I can always open a studio of my own and teach. To be honest I'll have to one day anyway. It's not like I can be a sixty year old prima ballerina." She fiddled with the program in her hand. "But I want to dance professionally as long as I'm able. To leave because of injuries or age is one thing, but to leave to have a baby," she shook her head, "I don't think I can do it. Am I completely selfish?"

Evan studied her face and saw the war she was fighting with herself. She hadn't made this decision lightly. It was a sacrifice for her. He could tell by the pain in her eyes as she had spoken. "I don't think so. I think you're making a difficult decision the best you can." He grabbed her hand and gently caressed her knuckles. "If your husband wanted a family, would you be willing to discuss the possibility of adoption?"

Clara's eyes widened, and then she smiled brightly. "If he would be willing to consider adoption then I would be happy to go that direction. I guess I always figured guys would want to prove their virility or something. Adoption hadn't even crossed my mind."

"I think there are plenty of guys who would be open to the idea of adoption, but it's probably something you'd want to discuss early on in the relationship – like you have with me."

Clara looked down at their still intertwined hands. "That's exactly why I brought it up now. I didn't want you to choose me at the end if this was going to be problem for you." She laughed self-consciously. "Not that I think I'm a shoo-in or anything. The other girls are amazing and you're just as likely to pick them, but I wanted everything out on the table."

"I appreciate that." He looked at her questioningly before continuing. "Now I have a question for you. I'm a football coach and while I can find a school in New York to teach at easily enough, my dream is coaching at the college level one day. Would you be willing to follow me if I got an offer in some small town in the middle of nowhere?"

Clara pulled her hand back. "That would be difficult. I don't know if I would or not. I've worked so hard for my position."

Evan tucked a curl behind her ear. "I'm just putting everything on the table. Like you said, I don't want to get to the end and find out that this is an issue you can't compromise on. I understand how hard you've worked, and how difficult it would be to leave it behind."

The music began for the next act, and they both turned to face forward, their attention grabbed by the music and dance presented for their enjoyment. Near the end of the performance, Clara leaned over and whispered, "If I loved a man deeply, I would follow him anywhere – even if that meant I'd be leaving my dream job behind. Especially if it would be helping him attain his dream. I had my chance. It's only fair he gets a chance, too."

Evan smiled at her and squeezed her hand gently. He had honestly expected her to say that she wouldn't ever leave her career behind for anyone. After all, her mother had sacrificed so much, and she had worked so hard to attain it. He wouldn't blame her. To hear her say that she would be willing to leave it all behind for someone she loved made him feel an affection for her that he hadn't expected.

Following the performance there was a small reception. The younger children gathered around the cookies while the older ones accepted the bouquets of flowers and stood with their family members for pictures. Clara congratulated each child she passed, giving encouragement and praise. It wasn't until they reached the girl who had played the role of Clara that she was recognized.

"You're Clara Parker!" the girl squealed. "You're my role model. I want to be just like you when I grow up." The girl was also African-American like Clara. Evan didn't know much about ballet, but he knew that there were still not many principal ballerinas who were of that ethnicity. It had to be encouraging for an up-and-coming dancer to see someone who looked like her dancing in the spotlight.

At her enthusiastic greeting, others turned to look, and soon Clara was surrounded by admirers and taking her picture with the dancers. Evan stepped back and enjoyed watching the warmth she had for all of the performers. Regardless of age, skill, or ethnicity, Clara was sweet, friendly, and lavish with compliments to every child. The director of the performance came over to thank her profusely for coming to their little show.

Clara pointed at Evan. "You can thank him. It was his idea."

The director looked over, and her eyes widened. "Evan Garnett! One of your dates is Clara Parker?" She smiled as she looked between the two. "Well, I know who I'm rooting for now." She straightened her clothes. "You know, they asked me to sign a release that they could use parts of the show for a program on television, but I was so distracted by the performance I didn't even give it more than a glance before I signed it. Oh my!"

Before they left, Evan saw Penny darting to the director. He was certain she was giving her instructions on not giving away details about the show before it aired, probably reminding her that it was in the papers she had signed (whether she had actually read them or not), and possibly threatening with a lawsuit should she not comply. The director nodded enthusiastically, and then hurried off to the parents, most likely to relay the message to them.

Evan thought about Clara on the way home. She was quiet, staring out the window, and he wondered if she was thinking about him as well. He had liked her, and that feeling went deeper after she admitted that she would follow him abandoning her dream job – *if* she loved him. Would Eliana be willing to do that for him?

"Thank you for a wonderful evening," Clara said when they got back home. "The weird thing about this show is that we get one date, and that's not long enough for someone like me to fall deeply in love. But I feel like you're someone I could fall in love with." Reaching up, she cupped his cheek with her hand. "I enjoyed being with you." Softly, she kissed his cheek, and then walked away.

She was right. This was no way to pick a wife. One date wasn't nearly enough to make a decision like that. How was he supposed to know? Clara was lovely, and he enjoyed being with her, but then again, so was Robyn, and Marian, and so many others.

He yanked off his tie feeling frustrated by the whole process, the show, the dates, everything. Marching out to the cottage he pounded on the door. A disheveled Eliana answered looking like she had crawled out of bed. For a moment he felt bad, remembering that she was sick, but his frustration won out.

"Would you leave your dream job and follow me wherever God leads?" he asked without preamble.

Eliana blinked slowly as if trying to compute what he had asked. "I take it Clara would," she responded softly.

"*If* she loved me deeply, but how is she supposed to know that with only one date?"

Leaning against the door jamb, Eliana answered, "You both knew the pattern of the show before you signed the contract."

He raked his fingers through his hair feeling defeated. "I just didn't think it would be so hard."

"If it makes you feel better, there are a few days between the last date and the finale. You can date any of the girls over again and without the cameras around. It's still not long enough, but an engagement isn't the same as a marriage."

Evan looked at her closely. Even with her hair mussed up, and no make-up, she was still beautiful to him. "Do you want me to find another girl? What about us?"

Eliana let out a humorless laugh. "You were the one who came to me accusing me of various things, wanting to know how to choose. You're the one who has twelve other choices right now. I'm trying to keep myself from getting my heart broken, okay?" Her eyes teared up, but she kept her emotions in check.

Sighing, Evan gestured helplessly. "I'm sorry, Eliana. Here you are sick, and I've come up to vent my frustrations to you." He paced outside her door. "I just don't know what to do."

"Unfortunately, I don't know either. But I've been praying for you all day that God will let you know who to pick."

"I suppose I should be praying the same thing," he replied with rueful smile. "He knows best, right?"

"Right. Are you better now? Because if I'm going back to work tomorrow, I need to get more rest."

"I'm better. Thanks. Feel better." He turned away and heard the door close quietly behind him. "Lord, I need Your wisdom if I'm going to do this. Please lead me."

A vibration in his pocket told him he had a text. *Mom loves Yi for the bracelet, but I'm still rooting for Robyn or Sarah.*

Another vibration alerted him to Scott's text. *Too artsy. Pick Robyn the recruiter.*

Evan shook his head as he pocketed the phone. It must be nice for this to be so cut and dried for everyone else.

Maybe one day, he'd have a clear answer, too.

Clara Parker's Post-date interview

"Evan is just the kind of guy I could picture myself with. He's thoughtful, understanding, and considerate. I would love to get to know him better."

The 10th Date

Pre-date interview with Emma Laird

"Evan and I have a lot in common. We're both from Iowa, both enjoy sports, and both coach. I think we might really click over those things." Emma's dark brown hair was pulled back into a ponytail which made her emerald green eyes really pop. Tall and athletic, she made Eliana feel frumpy. Then again, she wasn't fully recovered from her illness yet, and felt sort of 'blah' anyway.

Emma was right though. She and Evan were completely compatible on paper. Penny thought that Emma was going to end up with Evan's heart. She could barely control her excitement over this date. Eliana on the other hand only felt dread. This could go really well for Evan – which in turn would not be great for her. Still she'd known all along that it was a possibility. Why had she let herself fall for him? She nearly snorted aloud. 'Let herself'. That was funny. She was long gone before she had even realized what was happening.

Evan was waiting in the foyer wearing an Iowa Hawkeyes t-shirt and jeans. "I was told to dress 'sporty' today. What does that even mean?" he said as Eliana approached.

"You look great," she assured him.

"I'm glad you're back." He lowered his voice so that

only she could hear him. "I missed having you around yesterday." He looked at her face closely. "You look better than you did last night."

"Thanks, I think." She smiled wanly. "I still don't feel fantastic, but better than I did. I'll probably be sitting a lot to rest today."

"Probably a good idea." He raised his hand as if to touch her, then immediately lowered it.

"Emma's ready!" Penny bounded up excitedly. "You're going to love her!"

Evan's eyes flicked to Eliana before he smiled at Penny. "I'm looking forward to seeing her again."

After making sure the crew was set, Eliana called for action. Emma walked in wearing an Iowa State Cyclones shirt, and the expression on both of their faces was comical. Eliana bit her lips to keep from laughing.

"Well, I guess when I was talking about our similarities I didn't take into account our college team preferences. This could be awkward," Emma said with a nervous chuckle.

"I think I can overlook your poor choice in schools," Evan responded with a twinkle in his eye.

Emma didn't seem terribly amused. "My 'poor choice in schools' is my employer. I'm a track and field coach at Iowa State University."

"Okay, things just got incredibly awkward. I'm so

sorry. I definitely stuck my foot in my mouth."

"You didn't know." Emma looked ready to put the whole thing in the past, and possibly wishing she could start over. "Let's get going. We don't want to miss our flight."

"Flight?" Evan looked over at Eliana for clarification, but she only smiled in return. She knew he'd enjoy this date, even if he and Emma didn't immediately hit it off like Penny had hoped.

******

The plane was chartered so the only ones on board belonged to the show besides the flight crew. Evan settled himself next to Emma determined to make up for his beginning blunder. A quick look around the plane showed him that Eliana was sitting a couple rows in front of him with a neck pillow on, already seeming to be asleep. It was the best thing for her to help recovery.

"Again, I'm so sorry about what I said earlier," he said turning his attention back to Emma.

"Don't worry about it. Let's start over." Emma smiled even if it seemed a little tense.

He did feel bad. His form about her had only said that she was a track and field coach at a university, but hadn't specified which university. Perhaps he should have known that she would be wearing the shirt representing her school, but he hadn't thought about it. "So what part of track and field do you specialize in."

"I'm a high jumper. I actually competed in the Olympics in high jump."

"Oh yeah! Now I recognize you. You took home a bronze, and had a couple commercials."

Emma smiled broadly at his recognition. "Yeah, I did. I'm surprised you remember. Once the Olympics are over most of us sink back into anonymity. Only the ones who win multiple gold medals seem to reach true celebrity status."

Fidgeting with the arm of his seat, Evan admitted, "Well, I sort of remember you because I thought you were really pretty. I know, it's shallow."

"Or maybe it's flattering."

"So where are we going that we need to fly to get there?" Evan's curiosity could no longer be kept back.

"I wanted it to be a surprise, but I guess you can know now. We're going to the Las Vegas Bowl."

"What? Are you serious?" Evan couldn't believe it.

"I know it's not a bowl that Iowa – or Iowa State – plays in, but maybe that's a good thing." She grinned at him. "I'd hate for us to have our first fight already."

"I love college football! I've always wanted to go to a bowl game. I don't care who's playing."

"This show has come up at a bad time then with all the bowl games going on," Emma teased.

"I may have been recording them and watching them at night," he admitted with a grin.

"I've been watching them myself," she admitted. "Did you see that crazy come-from-behind victory by Arizona?"

Now that they were speaking his language, Evan and Emma chatted easily through the rest of the flight. They compared teams, talked about upsets, and reveled over incredible plays. He was impressed at her knowledge of the game. She was obviously a fan of the sport, not simply trying to impress him.

"So do you enjoy all sports?" he asked. "Or do you have a few favorites?"

"I pretty much enjoy watching them all, but working at ISU I tend to like college sports best, and I particularly enjoy football and basketball. Aside from track and field, of course."

The pilot announced that they were going to begin their descent. Evan looked out the window, watching the hotels of the strip come into view.

"Have you ever been to Vegas before?" Emma asked.

Evan shook his head. "Nah. It's not really someplace I've been eager to go, but I'm excited about the football game."

Emma laughed. "I came once with a girlfriend who wanted to do Vegas for a bachelorette party. It's not really my type of place. I don't drink, or gamble, so I stuck to enjoying the food and shows."

They all disembarked and went straight to the stadium. Evan enjoyed the atmosphere of excitement: the school bands, the cheerleaders, the media, the fans – it was exactly what he had expected and this was only one of the smaller bowl games. He couldn't imagine how much more exciting it would be to be at one of the bigger bowls. The seats they had were right on the fifty yard line. It was all perfect.

He and Emma looked over both teams' stats and chose who they would be rooting for. Soon the national anthem was played and the game began. It was a close match with the game being won by a field goal at the last second. Emma had asked him throughout the game about how he would handle certain situations – "Would you punt or go for it?" "Extra point or two point conversion?" "Do you keep the quarterback in after a second interception or take him out?" He enjoyed talking to her about what he would do, and seeing if the coaches thought along the same lines as he did.

Emma's enthusiasm was also enjoyable. She cheered loudly for the team they had chosen, and wasn't afraid to chastise the refs for a bad call. He was impressed again with her knowledge of the sport and its rules. He was surprised she still had a voice after all the yelling.

After the game, Emma went to use the restroom, and Evan took the opportunity to find Eliana. "I need to change my date plans for tonight," he said quickly.

"I thought you might want to." She handed him a list she had compiled of shows, concerts, and restaurants in Las Vegas.

"Wow. You know me really well."

She shrugged. "Emma had wanted to keep the bowl game a surprise so you had no idea where you were going to be."

He looked over the list and found a restaurant by a celebrity chef. "No show will top that game, and I don't think I can fake enthusiasm for any of them right now."

Eliana turned to Penny and told her to get it set up. "We have some space at the MGM Grand where you guys can refresh and get changed."

"Right. Thanks for thinking of everything."

She smiled slightly. "It's my job."

He turned to leave, but then remembered something. "Oh, and ten?"

"Lords a-leaping," she filled in.

He smiled. "Laird the leaping high jumper. She was good. Did you see her at the Olympics?"

"No, I was on a project."

"That's too bad. She was worth watching." He saw her eyes narrow slightly, and for the first time thought he detected some jealousy. He knew it shouldn't make him happy, but it did. She was so careful to keep her feelings close to her chest except when he forced her to reveal them. It was lovely to see her crack a little.

Emma came back while he was still with Eliana. She

looked between the two for a moment, and he wondered if she saw something between them. It was only then that he realized how close he was standing to Eliana. He took a step back, and hoped he didn't seem guilty.

"I needed to change plans for tonight since I had no idea we would be in Vegas for our date," he explained.

"Oh of course." She seemed relieved at such a simple explanation at seeing him with the director.

Eliana spoke up. "For now, we'll get you guys to the MGM Grand where you can change clothes and freshen up if you'd like."

Emma stepped closer to Evan. "That would be wonderful."

Evan was aware of the tension between the two women on the way to the hotel. They sat on either side of him, Eliana staring out the window with her back straight and shoulders tensed, and Emma had his hand clutched in a death grip, eyes straight ahead. He found it amusing that Emma was the only one of the twelve who had figured out where his interest was, and the only one who made Eliana uncomfortable.

When he arrived in the lobby that evening, Eliana was listening to Penny, but she didn't appear pleased. Her arms were folded across her chest, her jaw was tense, and she was looking around the lobby distractedly even though Penny was animated about her topic. He wandered in their direction, curious about what could be upsetting Eliana. Was funding being cut or did something go wrong with the filming this afternoon?

Penny had her back to him, and didn't see him approach. "I'm telling you Emma is perfect for Evan! Did you see the chemistry between them at the football game? I was right. She was the best option. I can't wait to see them tonight. It can only get better." Eliana looked over Penny's shoulder drawing her attention to the fact that he was there. Penny blushed. "I'm sorry, Evan. I didn't know you were there." She hurried off in embarrassment.

"So, she's a fan of Emma, huh?"

"Apparently."

He grinned. "Are you jealous?"

"No, of course not. You're supposed to pick one of these women. It would make sense for you to pick Emma. You have a lot in common, and she's very pretty." Evan held up a hand to stop her flow of words.

"You're only telling me what you've been rehearsing to yourself." He stepped closer and lowered his voice. "But you've left something out. She's not you, and you are the one I love."

Eliana smiled softly and lowered her head. "But you shouldn't."

He shrugged. "There's nothing wrong with me loving you. It just didn't fit the script." He looked around quickly to make sure no one was paying attention before placing a quick kiss on her cheek. "No matter what happens, I love you."

There was a stir, and Eliana slipped back into her director role. The crew was ready, and Emma was on her way. "Thanks for playing your part convincingly," Eliana whispered before rushing off.

Evan moved to get in position, but was not prepared for Emma's loveliness. Her hair was down and framing her face in perfect curls. She wore a black dress that was perfect for a night out in Vegas, and her make-up drew attention to her brilliant green eyes.

"Wow," Evan breathed. "You look amazing."

Emma's face lit up in triumph, and Evan almost thought he saw her eyes flick over to Eliana for a brief moment. "Thank you. You clean up pretty good yourself."

The restaurant was within walking distance so they walked along the strip with Emma's arm tucked possessively through his. The restaurant was one of the nicest Evan had ever been in and the menu looked amazing. He was glad the show was paying for the date, because the prices were high although he was certain that it was worth the cost.

They relived the football game from that afternoon, argued about the chances for the Hawkeyes and Cyclones basketball teams for the year, and had a deep discussion about Iowa politics. Still Evan kept thinking that Emma felt like a good friend. He enjoyed being with her, but he didn't feel an attraction for her other than noticing that she looked very pretty. There was no urge to kiss her, or put his arm around her. Instead, he almost felt like they should have a secret handshake or a victory dance for touchdowns. She was on the same level as Scott in his mind.

"I've always wanted to watch the fountains at the Bellagio," she mentioned. "Do you think we have time for that before we go back home?"

He glanced at his watch. "Yeah, I think so." They paid for dinner and then wandered over to the famed area to watch the show. Evan noticed several of the crew clearing a place for them to stand which would give them a fantastic view and security taking their spots nearby. Fortunately, it seemed like most people were too excited and distracted to notice them. Eliana had positioned the cameras in a way that a casual observer would miss, although he was certain she wasn't sacrificing quality shots in the process.

The show was fun. Lights and Christmas carols synced perfectly with the fountains. People nearby oohed and ahed as they watched the display. Emma held tightly to his arm throughout the program, and Evan was amused to find that the only thought he had on her hanging on him like that was that it would be good for the television show.

After it was over, they all headed back to the airport and climbed on the plane to head back to L.A. Emma chatted about the fountains, and the food, but Evan felt drained. It wasn't long after takeoff that he drifted off. As they descended, he woke up suddenly, and Emma giggled next to him.

"I guess I wore you out today," she commented.

"I guess so. It was a busy day." He ran a hand over his face, and hoped he didn't look too mussed up. There was still the post-date interview to get through.

They entered the mansion with Emma characteristically clinging to his hand. She turned to face him with a large smile. "It was such a nice date," she said demurely.

"Well, you were the one who set it all in motion by getting the bowl tickets. Thanks again for that. I've always wanted to do that, and it was even more fun than I thought it would be."

She cocked her head to the side, and he knew that she was hoping for a kiss. Before he could think about it too much, he lowered his head and kissed her near her mouth. She looked up at him with some confusion, but then her gaze moved to where Eliana stood. She nodded and smiled sadly.

"Thanks for giving me a chance," she said with a hint of tears in her voice before she dashed out of the room.

Eliana came up next to him. "What was that about?"

"I think she knows who I would choose." His phone buzzed, and he grabbed it to see what the newest choice was for Kelly and Scott.

Jillian is cray-cray, Scott wrote.

My opinion is the same. Although I would have worded it much more eloquently, was Kelly's response.

"What was their opinion tonight?" Eliana asked. He

loved that she knew what the texts were about.

"They're sticking with Robyn or Sarah."

Eliana nodded. "Both are good choices."

He looked over at her. "Yet neither are the best choice."

Emma Laird's post-date interview

"It was fun, and I'm so glad I got the opportunity, but he's already in love with someone else. I just don't know if he knows it yet or not."

The 11th Date

Pre-date interview with Kaydence Ochoa

"I don't know what to think any more." Kaydence sat straight in the chair. Her shoulder length hair was thick and dark. Her eyes were dark as well with black eyelashes, her lips were full, and her bone structure was one that gave the feeling that she was descended from royalty. Her very air was elegant, but her brows were drawn down in confusion. "Everyone says that Evan is polite, a gentleman, that they had fun, but no one seems to think he'll pick them at the end. Is it possible that he's gotten to the end of this and has no preference yet? It doesn't make sense."

Eliana sighed. Torn between happiness that none of the women seem to think Evan has fallen for them, and frustration that the show may lack chemistry which could end up ruining it all, she didn't know what to think either. Maybe she should have chosen someone else instead of Evan. Yet she knew that he was a man that would appeal to nearly everyone. No one else had impressed her nearly as much.

And that was part of the problem. She knew others would fall for him, because she had. How could this possibly end in a way that didn't break her heart?

******

Only two dates left, Evan thought as he waited for Kaydence. This whole project had started taking a toll on him. Sleep was getting more difficult to obtain as he stressed about the finale. What was he supposed to do? Pick one of these girls only to have them figure out that his heart already belonged to the director? It wasn't going to end pretty.

He raked his hand through his hair as he sighed. It was time to get his head back in the game. Two more dates. Then he had a couple of days to figure it all out. It would all work out. *Please, God, let it work out.*

He must have missed the call for action, because he was suddenly aware of Kaydence's presence in the room. She carried herself like a princess even though she wore jeans and a Disney princess t-shirt. He had to admit she was lovely, but she looked hesitant. He wondered what the women had been saying about him to make her unsure of him.

"What's the plan today?" he asked with a smile.

"We're going to Disneyland." A grin spread across her face as she shrugged. "I've always wanted to go, but never had the chance."

"Then Disneyland it is! Let's go." They climbed in the car. "So tell me what has prevented you from going to Disneyland?"

She sighed and leaned back against the seat. "First it was money. My dad emigrated from Mexico when he was little and worked hard, but there was never a lot of extra money. He met my mom in high school and they married as soon as they graduated and proceeded to enlarge their family."

"Big family I assume?"

"Oh yes! My dad was a devout Catholic so we became the stereotypical Mexican-American family, I guess. There were twelve of us kids including two sets of twins."

"Wow! That is a large family. Where do you fit in?"

"I am the sixth of twelve and came between the two sets of twins." Kaydence turned to face him. "It would have been easy for me to get lost in the chaos, but I wasn't going to let that happen. I found that I was good at music, and I poured everything into it. A lady at a church offered to give me free lessons as long as I worked hard, and I did." Evan pulled into the Disneyland entrance. The producers had arranged for them to arrive before the park opened so they were able to get right in. Kaydence's eyes sparkled as she looked around her. "I fell in love with the flute although I started with piano. My life has been so focused on music that I've nearly forgotten what it's like to have fun. I went from my private lessons to college to playing in a symphony. One day I woke up and realized that I never really had a childhood to speak of."

"Well, let's start a second childhood today," Evan suggested. "It shouldn't be too difficult here."

They parked and took the tram to the entrance. Kaydence eagerly took in everything, snapping pictures at the normal landmarks: the train station with Mickey's face in flowers, the castle, the giant Christmas tree, and with any character they could find. Evan enjoyed watching her dive in so enthusiastically. He took pictures of her whenever possible. This was a day that should be documented so she could look back on it.

They rode every ride they came to from the Alice in Wonderland ride to Thunder Mountain. Their conversation was fun and lighthearted. They debated which of the princess movies was the best classic, talked about the gems that were found amongst the non-princess movies, compared Pixar favorites, and the future of Marvel and Star Wars. He loved hearing her scream on Space Mountain, her laughter on the tea cups, and her enthusiasm on the Jungle Cruise. She bought them matching mouse ears, and they proudly wore them throughout the park.

At one point, Kaydence slipped away to get a Dole Whip, and Evan took the opportunity to approach Eliana. "What am I supposed to do for my date? I can't take her away from here before closing. She's having way too much fun."

"I've got it taken care of," Eliana assured him. "I kind of figured that something this big would need to be an all-day event."

"Could have told me," Evan grumbled though he smiled at her.

"She wanted to surprise you." She handed him a slip of paper. "Here's the information on your part of the date. If you want to change anything let me know as soon as you can."

"Thanks." He slipped it into his pocket certain that everything would be perfect. "By the way, good job on having a flautist as the pipers piping."

Eliana's lips twitched. "Well, it was either that or a plumber. There were some lovely plumbers, but Kaydence beat them all."

Evan laughed heartily as he moved to rejoin Kaydence. They continued to make their way through the park until it was time for dinner. Evan had used a moment when Kaydence had slipped into the restroom to read the plans for that night. As he had suspected, it was perfect. Eliana had a flair for this.

At dinner, Evan took her to Blue Bayou where they were served a three course meal. Her eyes lit up as each course came. She closed her eyes to savor each first bite. He could almost see her soaking in every moment of the day.

Following dinner they were given VIP seats to watch *Fantastmic!* Kaydence grabbed his arm as the story unfolded. Awe was written on her face as she watched the show filled with characters and special effects. If this was the start of her second childhood, she was diving in with enthusiasm.

After a few more rides, they gathered near the castle to watch the fireworks. Eliana had gotten them a reserved spot for that as well. He put his arm around Kaydence as they watched the show set to Christmas carols. It was the perfect end to a fun day.

On the way home, Kaydence sighed happily, her eyes closed as her head rested against the car seat. “That was the best day!”

“I hope it’s only the beginning of your second childhood,” Evan mentioned. “Everyone should have a chance to cut loose and have fun every once in a while.”

“You’re right. I’ll try to remember that all work and no play isn’t any better for Kaydence than it was for poor Jack.” She shifted and looked at him. “Can I ask you something?”

“Sure.” Evan wondered at the hesitancy in her voice. They’d kept to light topics all day. Apparently she had something serious to discuss before they ended their night.

“This is completely off the record. I won’t tell anyone.” She placed her hand over the camera that had been installed in the dash of the car. “They won’t air this if there’s no picture – hopefully.” She lowered her voice and he knew she was attempting to make it too difficult to decipher what she was saying on the recording as well. “Are you in love with someone already? I mean, someone who isn’t part of the twelve?”

Evan’s heart raced. Should he be honest? He glanced over at her and knew he couldn’t lie. “Yes, but I fell in love with her after this project started so I couldn’t get out of it.”

Kaydence smiled slightly. “We’ve been wondering.”

When he went to speak, she raised her hand. “I know. I promised not to tell anyone, and I won’t.” She leaned forward and whispered, “Is it Eliana Santos?”

Evan couldn’t stop the smile that filled his face. Knowing that the women had figured things out, even down to whom it was that he already had feelings for, made things a little easier. He knew he wasn’t going to break any of their hearts. In answer to her question, he simply gave a little nod.

“I thought so. In case you don’t know, she is completely in love with you, too. You can see it in the way she watches you.” Kaydence removed her hand from the camera signaling the end of their private conversation.

They arrived back at the mansion. As they parted for the night, Kaydence smiled up at him brightly. “Thank you for a memorable day.” She gave him a hug and whispered in his ear, “I hope you get the woman who holds your heart.” Placing a sisterly kiss on his cheek, she left him.

Evan couldn’t help but smile as he watched her leave. It was nice to have at least one person who knew the truth.

As if they knew his date was over, he got two texts from Kelly and Scott nearly simultaneously.

Kirstin seemed – nice, Kelly wrote vaguely. *I’m still a big fan of Robyn or Sarah.*

Another one bites the dust. Move on to the next! Scott wrote.

He didn’t respond. Both he and Kirstin knew that there

was no future for them. After all, she had met someone else. For that matter so had he. That was an easy decision for both of them.

Kaydence Ochoa's post-date interview

"That was a truly magical day that I will never forget, and I'm so glad I spent it with Evan. As for a future between us," she shrugged, "that might only be a dream."

The 12th Date

Pre-date interview with Harmony Lancaster

"I know Evan and I are going to have a great time today regardless of what his final decision is. Everyone who has been out with him has come back completely excited, and saying they had the best time." Harmony wasn't a person who looked like she belonged with Evan. Her dark hair had bright pink tips, her eye make-up around her light blue eyes was heavy and dark, fingernails painted black. She wore a band t-shirt with ripped jeans. Eliana knew that she was intelligent, sweet, and personable, and that Evan's high school students would think she was incredibly cool as well.

Eliana was relieved that it was the final date. The sooner all this was over, the better. She was tired of seeing Evan go on all these dates, tired of making sure that each woman looked like the best candidate for him.

The producers on the other hand were ecstatic. The viewers loved the show. Social media groups were popping up for each woman, people were choosing favorites. There was talk of having a reunion show next Christmas to catch up with everyone, particularly Evan and his lucky woman.

And any of them would be lucky to be chosen by him. Not lucky, she corrected herself. Blessed. Incredibly blessed to have such a great guy by their side, to watch him succeed in his career and comfort him when things got rough, to have his support as she pursued her own dreams.

All of a sudden, she could picture it clearly. She saw herself cheering at high school football games, taking videos, and making highlight reels for the boys to send to prospective colleges. She saw Evan coming with her or meeting her during school breaks at exotic locations while she directed an upcoming movie. There would be a little house in Merryton waiting for their return. When he got a position at a university – which she knew would happen eventually – she would pull back and only do movies that really intrigued her. And while she slowed down, they would have their own children, maybe two, three at the most, and she would direct the videos of their lives, all while supporting Evan and his team.

The clarity in which all of that hit her was so startling that she sat down. She could see it, and it would work. All of the debate about whether she could live in Iowa or whether he could travel with her no longer mattered. That was the life she wanted. Yes, she wanted to direct, but she was certain they could mesh their careers into a happy life.

God, what do you want me to do? He's supposed to choose another woman in a few days. Do I tell him this or wait and see what You accomplish? If it's Your will, surely You will work it out in an amazing way, right? Eliana wished God would speak out loud on this topic, but the heavens appeared to be silent for now. She sighed and stood up. While she waiting for God, she had a job to do. One more date to get through.

******

Harmony bounded towards Evan with enthusiasm that made him smile. “I’m so glad to get a day with you myself!” she enthused. “Everyone has spoken so highly of you, I couldn’t wait to have my turn.”

“I’m glad to be with you as well. Should we get started?” Evan gestured towards the door, and Harmony took the lead. They drove to Eaton Canyon Natural Area where Harmony strapped on a backpack and led the way to a trail marked ‘waterfall’.

“I can carry that,” Evan offered, reaching for the backpack, but Harmony pulled away with a smile.

“I’ll carry it on the way up, and I’ll let you carry it back.” When he started to argue, she simply smiled, and retorted, “My date, my rules.” Then she began hiking again.

Evan shook his head, but followed. Soon he was entranced by her knowledge of the area, the different plants, and the stories she had to share. She was a gifted storyteller, and he often laughed at her tales. Every once in a while she would pull out their water bottles so they could hydrate before continuing.

When they reached the waterfall, they sat down and took in the beauty of the area. Harmony pulled out a couple of oranges, a bag of trail mix, and their waters. While they snacked, Harmony said, “This was where I composed my first song.”

"Really? This is a beautiful spot to compose."

Harmony chuckled. "I wasn't really feeling inspired by the beauty that day. My boyfriend had broken up with me, and I was angry. I wrote my feelings down in the form of a poem, but before I was done, I could hear the music that would go with it. When I got home, I wrote the chords to go with it, called my band up, and we spent the next several hours playing it. It had a wicked drum part."

"Are you still with that band?"

"Yeah, we've stuck together. Our parents are incredibly surprised. They figured we were just going through a phase." She laughed. "Maybe disappointed is a better word for our parents' reaction. Mine were hoping I'd do something more 'useful' with my life." She used her fingers to make air quotes.

Evan shifted on the rock to look at her more closely. "How does your band do?"

Harmony shrugged. "We get gigs fairly regularly, but we haven't been 'discovered' yet. We've paid to make a few CDs and sell them at our events when they let us." She looked at him with stars in her eyes. "But I'd rather live paycheck to paycheck playing drums with my band than be working in a boring office somewhere and making the big bucks, ya know?"

"I think it's great that you can do what you love, and that you're doing well enough to not need a second job to supplement tells me that you're more successful than you're letting on." She flushed under his praise, and he wondered how often she had been asked when she was going to grow up and get a real job.

"Not everyone sees it that way," she replied softly, confirming his suspicions.

"It seems like you're doing exactly what you're supposed to be doing." He stood up and brushed himself off. "Ready to head back?" He held out his hand for the backpack which she willingly relinquished this time.

They chatted more as they drove back towards the mansion, stopping at a diner where they both got a big hamburger and a mound of French fries. Evan had been eating at upscale places so long now that the greasy diner food seemed to taste amazing with its comforting quality.

By the time they got back to the mansion, Evan felt like he and Harmony had a good rapport. He was certain that she trusted him which seemed to be a huge thing for her. And it was a good thing, seeing as he had a huge surprise for her that night.

After Harmony walked away from him, and the cameras stopped rolling, he sidled up by Eliana. "Twelve drummers drumming?" he said in a low voice.

Her lips twitched. "She seemed ideal."

When he showed back up that evening, he felt a little ridiculous, but they had assured him that he was dressed appropriately. Faded, ripped jeans, a t-shirt that felt like it was a size or two too small, and a brown leather jacket with canvas tennis shoes were apparently the right thing to wear to this event.

Harmony's face lit up when she saw him, so they must have known what they were doing. "You look great! Don't look so 'teacherish' now." She giggled at his affronted look.

"I guess I'm glad you're pleased, although I have a feeling it's not enough. Everyone will wonder why you are stuck with a boring guy like me."

Harmony blushed again and smoothed her skirt. She wore ripped black leggings with a red and green plaid, pleated skirt, black boots and a red sweater. "It seemed Christmasy."

He drove her to a club – not really in his comfort zone, but it was necessary for his surprise to work. Harmony smiled as they went inside. "This doesn't seem like you," she commented, raising her voice to be heard over the thumping music provided by the deejay.

"To be honest, it's not, but I think I'll still enjoy the night."

"Wanna dance?" Before he could answer though, someone touched Harmony's shoulder. She turned around and shrieked in joy as she hugged the person who had interrupted. "What are you doing here?"

"We've got a gig tonight," the young woman replied. She was short with blonde curls streaked with the same hot pink that colored Harmony's hair. Behind her were a tall African-American girl with braided hair and another girl with honey blonde long hair, both having the same pink tints.

Harmony's face fell. "You have a gig without me? Who's your drummer?"

The African-American girl held out some drumsticks. "We were hoping you would join us."

Harmony looked up at Evan in indecision. "I can't. I'm here with Evan."

Evan leaned in to speak in her ear. "You're here for this. I want to hear your band play, and they wanted their drummer for the night. It worked out pretty well, I think."

Harmony's face lit up with joy. "You really want to hear us?"

"Absolutely! Now, go join your band."

Not needing any more prompting, Harmony left. Evan found a spot where he could see the small stage area and ordered a soda.

"Ladies and gentlemen, please welcome a club favorite band – Pink Aftermath!" The crowd cheered at the deejay's announcement.

Harmony's band came out and took their places. She had changed into hot pink pants and a white t-shirt. All of the band members wore pink and their instruments were white. The curly haired blonde took front and center stage as the lead singer, and also had a guitar. The other blonde played keyboard while the final girl played bass.

The band launched into a song they called *Tell Him* about life being short and not wanting to miss out on an opportunity because they were too afraid to say something. Evan was impressed at the musical ability the band displayed. He turned to see if Eliana was impressed only to find that her face had paled. Immediately he wondered if her illness had returned. He wanted to get up and check on her, but then she turned to face him. She smiled softly, but it was enough to ease his doubts. Reaching up, she scratched by her ear, and his heart rate sped up. She had never before asked for him to meet her. He had always instigated their meeting before. Realizing he hadn't responded yet, he cupped his chin, and turned back to face the stage.

The rest of the evening was a blur for him. All he could think about was spending time with Eliana afterwards. It wasn't fair to Harmony, but somehow he thought she would understand if she knew. Besides she was in her element up on the platform, beating her drums.

When he had contacted the lead singer of Pink Aftermath to ask if they could arrange a gig for their date, she had been ecstatic. After all, this would give them national coverage, and a really good opportunity to be seen by possibly an agent or producer. It might lead to bigger and better things, and he sincerely hoped it would.

Their farewell was simple when they got home. Harmony thanked him for the surprise, gave him a hug, and disappeared. It was almost as if she knew he had somewhere to be.

******

Eliana rehearsed what she might say to Evan on the

walk to the art studio. Nothing seemed right. She didn't want to influence him, but she wanted to present her side. She didn't want to make things even more difficult, but knew that what she said may present another complication.

Pausing outside of the studio, she lifted her eyes to the night sky. The mansion was far enough from the city that stars were actually visible. "God, I think this is what you want me to do, but I don't know what to say. Please give me wisdom." Feeling more confident and peaceful, she entered.

Evan crossed to meet her as soon as she stepped inside, his eyes lit with anticipation. He grasped her hands. "I feel like it's been ages since you signaled you wanted to meet me. I couldn't wait for the date to be over."

Eliana smirked. "Poor Harmony. That's not very complimentary."

He lowered his head although he smiled. "I guess not, but I don't know. I get the feeling that they're figuring out who it is that I'm most interested in." He rubbed his thumb across her knuckles and Eliana felt a shiver go up her spine in response. "What did you want to see me for?"

Eliana took a deep breath and extracted her hands from his. She couldn't think clearly when he was touching her. Beginning to pace, she told him, "I was listening to Harmony's band's song – the one about telling him because life is short, and I realized that I needed to tell you something."

Concern in his eyes, he took a step closer to her. "What?"

With her hands locked in a death grip, Eliana forced herself to stop pacing and look him in the eyes. "This morning I had a revelation, and I wasn't sure if I should tell you or not, so I asked God, but He didn't seem to have an answer right then. But then that song started to play, and I felt like He was answering me." Swallowing hard, she continued. "Evan, I know that when we've talked about 'us' location has been an issue, but I know we can make it work. I'll be by your side helping the boys get their highlight reels ready for scouts, and you can come with me when I need to travel for work whenever school's not in session. We can do it."

Passion and uncertainty warred in his eyes as he closed the gap between them. "What about the show?"

"I don't know," she whispered. "Maybe you can pick one who would be okay with being a short term diversion."

"That doesn't seem fair to her, or you, or me." He lifted a hand and gently caressed her cheek. "Eliana, I want to be with you, and I want the world to know it."

She leaned into his hand, closing her eyes, savoring his touch. Then his phone dinged, and her eyes flew open. She knew it would be his sister and friend with their opinions of that night's program. Sighing, she asked, "What did they think tonight?"

He glanced at the messages. "Both of them really like Marian, although Scott still is rooting for Robyn solely on the basis that he thinks boys would want to play for us with her around. Kelly has added Marian to her list of potential candidates which include Robyn and Sarah."

Eliana moved over to the sofa and sat down at the edge, hands between her knees. "You've been with all of them now. If there weren't the complication of – well, me – who would you pick?" She watched him intently as he came to join her. He was obviously taking her question seriously, thinking through everyone.

"Robyn is a favorite of mine. Marian was sweet. Clara was amazing. Kaydence was a lot of fun. I guess they would be my final four, but I don't have one that stands out over the others from those."

Eliana nodded. "You have four days before we film the finale live. Spend time with those four, pray for direction, and follow God's leading."

Evan looked over at her. "Will you pray for me, too?"

Not able to help herself, she ran her hand through his hair. "I already am." Kissing him tenderly on the cheek, she got up and left, content that God was in control.

Post-date interview with Harmony Lancaster

"I can't believe he surprised me with my band and a gig! It was so much fun to get to show him our music, and I know he enjoyed it, too. But I can't say that he was anything other than polite. I wonder who it is that he's already fallen for."

Intermission

It felt amazing to wake up knowing that there would be no cameras following him around all day, no dates to go on, no tension. Evan stretched in his bed, savoring the moment. Unfortunately, he soon remembered that there was still that one pesky thing he still needed to do – figure out what he was going to do for the finale.

Although Eliana had urged him to spend time with the four women he had mentioned to her, Evan knew he needed a little space to think. The days had been filled with busyness, dates, commotion, and stress. He needed a day alone, even without Eliana. Being with her would only confuse him more.

He went to the gym in his wing and worked out, took a long leisurely shower, watched some football, and most importantly, spent time in prayer and studying God's Word. Pulling out his 'game plan' he smiled. He had given each of them a chance, and he felt like he really did try to make a connection with them. Even with his final four choices, he somehow knew that there wasn't enough spark between them, although he was certain that was at least partially his fault. He couldn't give them his heart, because it already belonged to someone else. Even with that though, he felt like all four of them already understood that.

He ripped that page off of his pad, and started a new

game plan. He only had three days left. They needed to be used wisely if he was going to be ready for the finale.

Kelly and Scott sent their usual texts. Kelly added Clara to her growing list of potential sisters-in-law, and Scott agreed that Clara was nice enough, but lacked Robyn's fire.

By the time he went to bed, he felt confident that he was prepared for the next few days. He fell asleep praying that God would direct and give wisdom.

The following day, he asked Robyn, Marian, Clara, and Kaydence to meet him in the living room. He knew it created a stir among the other women, and the crew. He caught a glimpse of Emma's disappointed face, and Sarah looked like she was struggling to hold back tears, and he felt badly, but they knew he could only pick one. Now it was up to him to decide who that one would be.

The four women sat on a large sectional couch while he took a recliner. He looked at their faces and tried to judge what they were thinking. Robyn looked friendly, Marian hopeful, Clara serene, and Kaydence confused. He took a deep breath and prayed that he would have the right words.

"I need your help," he plunged in. "There's only a couple days left until the finale, and you know I have a difficult decision to make. Of the twelve, I felt like I had the most connection with the four of you."

They smiled at him, and at each other. Marian clutched Robyn's hand.

"I need to know something from you though," he continued. "How do you feel about me?"

The rest immediately looked to Robyn. Her natural leadership took over and she seemed happy to lead the conversation. "Evan, you were wonderful to me. I think I could have easily fallen in love with you – except you were already in love before you ever got to me."

Kaydence spoke next. "You and I talked about this on the way home from our date. I haven't said anything to anyone else, but there's been a lot of speculating amongst all of us. You've been polite, kind, fun, a gentleman, everything we could hope for in a man, but you've been distant, and you and I both know why that is."

"You helped me live out a dream," Marian added. "And it was wonderful! But I felt like you were playing your part to perfection, not to please me, but to please someone else."

Clara looked around before adding her thoughts. "You are exactly the type of man I want to find one day, but it wasn't a perfect fit for us. You asked if I would leave New York, and I said I would if I really loved someone. Maybe one day I would love you that deeply, but after one date? I can't make a call like that."

Evan leaned forward. "So you see my dilemma. You are my top four, and none of you want to be with me."

Robyn smiled. "We may be your top four, but none of us are your 'one'."

Evan smiled slightly. "So how in the world do I make

a decision for the finale? Do I choose one of you and we both try to pretend like we have hope for the future when we both know we don't?"

The women all looked at each other, but no one spoke. Surprisingly, it was Marian who spoke up. "Give us a day to talk it over. Meet us back here tomorrow and we'll discuss it some more."

Evan knew he probably looked as disappointed as he felt, because as Robyn left, she whispered, "Cheer up, Champ. It'll be okay." He had been hoping to have everything resolved that day. There was limited time left to make a decision.

Heading back to his room, he spent the rest of the day in prayer and Bible study. He knew that only God could guide him in the right path on this.

The texts this evening made him smile.

Iowa St?! No way! Easy decision. Emma's out! Scott was emphatic.

What is it with boys and rivalries? You guys both love college football. Who cares which team? I'm adding her to my list, Kelly responded.

For a while his phone dinged and Scott and Kelly argued back and forth to his great amusement. He was still smiling when he went to sleep.

Two days left, and Evan was starting to feel a bit panicky. His game plan had started off so good, but stalled so quickly. Today would tell if the hesitation was enough to get the blockers to miss so he had a free run to the end zone, or if it gave them the opportunity to lay him out flat.

The four women were already waiting for him with big smiles on their faces. Kaydence held up her hands when he came in. “I want you to know that I didn’t tell them, but they guesed correctly.”

Evan shook his head in amusement.

“It wasn’t too hard to guess,” Robyn inserted. “The question we have for you is this: does *she* know?”

“Yes, she does, and she feels the same.” The women all squealed in delight at his announcement.

“Okay, we know what you’re gonna do,” Robyn continued. “But we’re going to need her assistant’s help.”

Marian went out to find Penny and bring her back while the others clued Evan in on their plan. When Penny came in she was stunned to find them all together with no sign of her favorite, Emma, but when they started explaining the situation to her, she was even more shocked. She sank down slowly onto the couch.

“How did I . . . but you . . . she never . . . Oh wait, that one time . . . oh no! . . . the producers . . . I just don’t . . .” her incoherent thoughts rambled on for a while, but the four women continued to press her. Evan sat back and watched these amazing women take charge. Each of them had a strength that he admired: Robyn’s leadership, Marian’s kindness, Clara’s grace, and Kaydence’s honesty. Together they were formidable and eventually not only wore down Penny’s defenses, but got her thinking that it was actually a good idea. She hurried off to do her part to make it happen.

Clara turned to Evan after Penny left. “Are you comfortable with this?”

“I think it’s how it has to be,” he answered. “I don’t see any other way.”

“Good!” Robyn stated. “’Cause we’re all out of ideas.”

Marian giggled. “It’s going to work out. I know it.”

“We’ve got things to do,” Clara reminded the rest. They bustled out the door chatting animatedly to each other.

Evan shook his head in wonder at the ease and wisdom of their decision. Wandering back to his room, he pulled out his game plan and marked some notes on it. Just like his game plans at home, they were in code so no one would know exactly what he had planned if they happened to find them. He praised God and thanked Him for laying out a plan.

Tomorrow was going to be busy doing one of his least favorite things – shopping. And shopping so close to Christmas only made it worse! Still, it would be worth it if everything went according to plan. His favorite four didn’t even know about this part of the plan, but he was certain they would love it.

As he was preparing for bed, his phone dinged. *Kaydence is a good one,* Scott surprisingly wrote. He’d been team Robyn for so long, it was weird to see him have another contender.

All Kelly wrote was, *YOU WENT TO DISNEYLAND WITHOUT ME?!*

The Finale

There was a peculiar energy in the house. Whisperings, speculating, and scheming seemed to be occurring under Eliana's very nose, but she couldn't figure out what was going on. She knew that Evan had taken her advice and met with his four favorites, but she didn't think he'd actually gone on dates with any of them. She also knew that tension was mounting. The women who hadn't been part of that sub-group looked like they were struggling to maintain the appearance that everything was okay – well most of them, Eliana amended as her eyes fell on Kirstin who was blissfully texting her new not-so-secret boyfriend.

Eliana had chosen the ballroom (yes, the mansion had a ballroom of all things) to have the finale in. A giant, gorgeously decorated Christmas tree sat next to an ornate fireplace with a fire crackling cheerfully. On the mantle were twelve stockings with each of the women's names on them. There were suspicious lumps in each one, and Eliana had no idea what Evan had planned.

The room was filled with people. A table with goodies and punch sat against the wall – it was Christmas Eve after all. What was strange, however, was that everyone was dressed up. It was odd seeing her cameramen in tuxes, the assistants and crew all dressed up in formal wear. Penny had rushed into her cabin two days earlier telling her that she had to dress up for the finale to celebrate the final episode. She had claimed that they were all going to do it, and looking around it was obvious she was telling the truth.

Eliana looked at the clock and felt her stomach clench. There was something nerve-wracking about a live show. If something went horribly wrong, she had only a few seconds to make a decision to try to salvage the show. Part of her was thankful for that additional stress though because it kept her mind off of Evan who looked so amazingly attractive in his tux.

Penny got the women lined up while Evan took his spot near the tree. Eliana double checked with the crew that everything was set before giving the signal to begin filming. The show began with a montage of clips from each date. The women and Evan were able to see this part on a large monitor. Evan stared at his feet through it all though, seeming a little nervous. The women nudged each other, grinned, and seemed pleased with the clips in general.

When finished Eliana nodded to Evan. He looked at the women and smiled charmingly. "I have been so blessed to get to meet each and every one of you ladies. My twelve dates of Christmas were wonderful, and I will never forget the time that I have spent with each of you. Unfortunately, I can only choose one. It was difficult, but there were four who I felt made a slightly bigger impact. But all of you have given so much to me that I have a Christmas gift for each of you. I hope that it will be something that will make you smile and think about me in the coming years." Evan stepped towards the mantle and pulled down Sarah's stocking.

Sarah stepped forward, a slight tremble visible in the movement of her white, lace dress. She swallowed hard and attempted to smile.

"Sarah, you are a sweet, and lovely woman. We had a rough start," Evan smiled at the remembrance, and even Sarah let out a soft laugh, "but ended the date well. Merry Christmas." He handed her the stocking and she reached inside. Pulling out a jewelry case, she opened it up and smiled while tears fell down her cheek. Inside was a delicate gold necklace with a pear shaped diamond.

"Thank you!" Evan came forward and clasped it around her neck. "It was so nice to be part of this. Thanks for not giving up on me immediately." She gave him a hug, then turned and gave the other ladies a hug as well, some of whom were fighting tears of their own, before she left the ballroom.

Eliana knew she would head to the living room where more treats were set up and a television was on so they could see how the rest of the show went. Hopefully by the end they would all be celebrating a successful show, and it wouldn't be too depressing in there.

"Paloma," Evan said next.

Unlike Sarah, Paloma stepped forward with grace and confidence. Eliana had a feeling that she had known immediately after her date that she and Evan wouldn't be together, and she was okay with that outcome. Her red, long sleeved dress was stunning, and Eliana was certain that there were some (men especially) who would be questioning Evan's decision here.

"You and I had a fantastic day together, but I think we both recognized that our ambitions led us in different directions. I admire you greatly, and wish you all the best. Merry Christmas." He handed her the stocking, and she eagerly reached in.

Looking up at him in surprise, she gasped, "You made a donation in my name to the turtle rescue organization. That is the best gift anyone could have given me." She hugged him tightly before saying goodbye to the other women and leaving the room.

Evan moved to Lisette's stocking, and she moved forward with a sad smile on her face. The sage green in her dress brought out the green tints in her hazel eyes which shimmered with tears.

"Lisette, you cook with love and make everything taste better because of it. I know you will make some man very happy, because of how happy you made me. I'll tell you right now, you were very close to be in my final group. I don't know if that helps or hurts," he said with a small smile, "but there was a connection that seemed to be missing. Merry Christmas."

Lisette reached into the stocking and laughed when she saw a salt and pepper shaker set that were porcelain chickens – one a bright red, and the other black. "I will think of you every time I use these." She pointed to the black chicken. "This one will be you, I think." When she hugged him she also kissed both cheeks, a heritage to her French roots. She proceeded to do the same with the women.

Evan skipped over Robyn's stocking to go to Yi's. She stepped forward looking elegant in a traditional Chinese dress that was a deep red with gold embroidery. "My mom will be yelling at her TV right about now," Evan said with a smile. "You won her heart with your generosity, and you taught me so much about art. But I don't think you felt any strong feelings towards me by the end of the night, and that's okay. I know that someday someone else will stir strong emotions in you, and you'll be thankful that you and I didn't work out. Merry Christmas."

Yi's stocking held a bag of gem stones that she could use in her jewelry. She smiled softly before she bowed slightly to him and then the ladies. Without a word, she left.

As Evan pulled Jillian's stocking she let out a sob. Eliana rolled her eyes even as she knew the producers would love the drama she was creating. Jillian rubbed her hands on her deep blue velvet dress.

"I don't think we got off to a great start, but we still managed to pull together a decent day. Still it was hard to recapture any hope for a future. Merry Christmas." His short speech told more than his words did. Jillian would have been the first one sent home in a different version of the show. There had never been any hope for her.

Still weeping, she opened her present, sobbing even harder when she pulled out a ceramic music box with geese painted on it. "Canadian geese are my favorite," she wailed as she threw herself into his arms. After a moment, he took her arms and gently extricated himself from her embrace, passing her to Robyn who rolled her eyes even as she helped move her along the line.

A breath of relief filled the room as Jillian left. Evan moved on to Kirstin's stocking. She stepped forward with a bounce in her step and a twinkle in her eyes which were challenged by the sparkle of her glittery blue dress.

"I know you will be just fine," Evan teased. "We knew early on that nothing was going to happen between us which allowed us to proceed straight to friendship. I wish you the very best, and I know you're in good hands. Merry Christmas." Eliana wasn't sure the audience would pick up on his cryptic comments, but everyone in the room knew about Kirstin's new boyfriend.

Reaching into her stocking, she pulled out a beautiful beach towel. She grinned as she held it against her. "I will be using this often," she promised.

"I know you will," he answered as he hugged her.

When she left, he passed over Marian's and Clara's stockings to Emma's. Emma stepped forward with her chin high, but hurt eyes. Her dress was gold while her necklace was garnets which seemed to be a tribute to Iowa State's colors.

"You gave me one of the best dates. I did not expect to get to go to a bowl game, and it's an experience I will never forget."

"Is this about the Iowa/Iowa State thing?" she asked,

her voice quivering slightly.

"No, I would never base my decision on something like that. I liked you, but felt more like you were a good buddy of mine instead of someone I could see myself marrying and settling down with. I hope you can forgive me. Merry Christmas."

Emma's hand trembled as she took the stocking. A program from the bowl game they attended that had been autographed by some of the players from both teams as well as both head coaches was inside. She smiled reluctantly. "I will definitely think of you whenever I see this," she promised. She walked out the door proudly without saying any goodbyes. Eliana was certain that she couldn't hold her fragile emotions together if she had and leaving with dignity was more important to her.

He grabbed Harmony's stocking last. She stepped forward with a smile. Her bright pink dress matching the color in her hair, the only one of the women not in a long gown. "You are incredibly talented. Don't forget that when times are hard. You are brave to pursue a difficult dream. Don't get discouraged. And your spunk is going to take you far, don't let anyone take it from you. Merry Christmas."

She grinned even more broadly when she pulled out pink drumsticks. She twirled them expertly in her fingers. "I'm glad we have a gig soon. I'm itching to use these." She gave Evan a hug and a kiss on the cheek before waving goodbye to the rest.

Four women were left, each grinning from ear to ear.

Eliana looked them over wondering which one Evan would finally choose.

"You four each hold a special place in my heart. I will remember you always, but I still have to say goodbye. Just know that I care about each of you deeply."

Evan moved on to Marian's stocking. She came over to him with her shell pink dress shimmering and her face glowing. "You were so enthusiastic during our date, so sweet and fun. I enjoyed being with you. You have to send me some of your cheese – or maybe someday I'll surprise you and pick some up. In any case, I think it is so cool that you are doing such an artisan work. Merry Christmas."

She gasped as she pulled out an autographed framed picture of Bradley Cooper. It was even personalized for her. "Are you kidding me? This is amazing!" She threw herself into Evan's arms and kissed his cheek. "You've been the best one-date-boyfriend I've ever had." Evan laughed as she went to tell the others goodbye.

Moving on, Evan grabbed Kaydence's stocking. "You and I probably had the best understanding of anyone. We were able to be open and honest with each other in a way I couldn't with anyone else. That's a valuable asset. I loved rediscovering our childhoods together at Disneyland, and I'll make sure that I see the wonder in things more now that I've been with you. Merry Christmas."

Kaydence teared up as she pulled out a photo album of their trip to Disneyland. "I'll never forget that day, and I'm determined that it is only the start of realizing that life is to be lived, not endured." She hugged him tightly. "Be happy."

With only two left, Evan picked Clara's stocking. Her white dress had a ballerina tulle skirt and made her look like a princess, an illusion only enhanced by her natural grace.

"We hit it off really well, and I think that given more time, we could have had something incredible. But without time, it was difficult to know exactly where we would go. You recognized that as well. I am so grateful that I was able to see not only your physical gracefulness, but the grace and humility you show with others. Merry Christmas."

Clara took a deep breath as she pulled a cast picture of the troop they saw perform *The Nutcracker*. The girl that had played Clara had written a small note that made her tear up when she read it. Hugging it to her chest, she said, "Thank you. This is a treasure." She lightly brushed her lips against his cheek before smiling and pirouetting out the door.

Evan grabbed the final stocking, and Robyn met him by the fireplace. Her deep purple dress flattered her figure and her complexion. She looked like royalty standing next to Evan with dignity. Eliana lowered her gaze. She wasn't sure she wanted to see the rest.

"Robyn, you are an amazing woman. We actually had a bit of a rough start like some of the others, but you recovered so magnificently that you won my respect. That and you showed me where to get the most amazing cupcakes in the world, so that boosted you up a lot, too."

She laughed. "You know it."

"You quickly became someone I counted on to take charge, to do things right, and to be honest with me. You thought about what I would like when you planned our date, and believe me, that was a rarity. I can see so many advantages to having you at my side. Merry Christmas."

Eliana didn't need to look up to know what was in Robyn's stocking. It would be a ring. Yet she couldn't help but watch so she saw the exact moment a stack of CDs was removed. They were recordings of the jazz band she and Evan had listened to, and they were autographed. Eliana wondered if the ring was in one of the CDs, and tried to signal to Robyn to open the cases, but she either didn't see her, or ignored her.

"There would be so many advantages to having you at my side, but one major disadvantage," Evan continued. Eliana held her breath. "I'm already in love with someone else."

Robyn hugged Evan and kissed him on the cheek before winking at Eliana who sat stunned in her chair. What was going on?

Before she knew it, Evan had grabbed her hand and pulled her over to the Christmas tree. Eliana smoothed the full skirt of her forest green dress and straightened the short green velvet jacket instinctively. Evan faced the camera. "I know this comes as a shock to you at home, but I don't think it surprises anyone who has been here.

Through the making of this show, I've gotten to know and spend time with Eliana Santos who has been our director. Although she warned me repeatedly not to, I fell in love with her. I didn't know what to do because I knew who I wanted to pick, and I knew who I was supposed to pick," he turned to face Eliana, "and the two didn't line up. So when I talked with my fave four," he grinned, "they cleared it all up for me. It wouldn't be fair to them, to me, or to you to pick one of them." Getting down on one knee, Evan pulled out a ring box from his pocket and opened it to show her a beautiful, antique-looking, diamond ring. "Eliana, I love you and you alone. Will you marry me?"

Eliana felt the tears slip down her face even as she nodded and laughed in pure joy. He placed the ring on her hand before pulling her tightly against him and kissing her passionately. Soon they were surrounded by the other women who were cheering happily, admiring her ring, and congratulating them both (some more sincerely than others). It was a better ending than Eliana could have dreamed up.

The Reunion Show

One year later

Martha Weatherby had been covering Hollywood's entertainment news for decades. It was a tribute to the success of the show that she had been brought on to interview them for the reunion show, but as Eliana watched her order people around, parade about the set as if she were the queen and they were all her lowly subjects, she had to wonder if it was worth it. Martha's face was freakishly smooth thanks to a recent botox injection or possibly a trip to the plastic surgeon. Her bleached blonde hair was sprayed into place so that Eliana was certain that not even hurricane force winds would move it.

"How are you doing?" Evan came up behind her and kissed her neck as he wrapped his arms around her waist.

Eliana took a deep breath. "I prefer being behind the camera," she admitted, "but I think this is going to be good."

Evan chuckled. "I would think you'd be used to it by now after the media frenzy we've been through the past year."

"You would think, but somehow it still amazes me. I prefer being at home in Merryton with you." She placed her hands over his, toying with the gold band on his left hand that had been designed by Yi Wang.

He lowered his head near her ear. "Mmm, I miss being home, too." He paused before asking. "You are happy there, aren't you?"

Eliana turned in his arms to face him. "I am extremely happy there. I figured you could tell that."

"Most of the time I know that, but when I'm back in Hollywood or on location with you, I can think that Merryton is pretty boring by comparison."

"Not boring. Comfortable," she corrected.

"All right people! I don't have all day!" Martha hollered.

Eliana rolled her eyes and was thankful she wasn't directing this program. In fact, the director looked like he was biting his tongue to keep from lashing out at the arrogant celebrity. As Eliana and Evan sat on a loveseat next to Martha's chair, she lowered her voice and said, "I hope you know that you are both just fleeting starlets. Don't think that this little program puts you in a class with the greats."

Evan's mouth twitched. "We wouldn't dream of it."

Martha glared and straightened in her chair. Eliana was sure that she was used to having people fawn all over her, but Eliana had worked with bigger celebrities than Martha, and Evan wasn't impressed by fame – except for maybe when it came to college football.

The director called for action, and Martha flashed her bleached white smile, ready to act as if she were the closest of friends with the couple next to her. "It's been one year since Evan Garnett shocked the nation by choosing, not one of the twelve lovely women who he had been on dates with, but the director of the series, Eliana Santos on the finale of *The Twelve Dates of Christmas*. Since then we have followed them through their engagement and were given a peak into their elopement this past summer. Now it's time to catch up with them as well as the twelve contestants on the show." She turned to Eliana and Evan. "Eliana, how has life in a small town in the Midwest been?"

"They've been very welcoming, and I've settled in, made friends, and love being near my husband." She squeezed Evan's hand. It was all true. Kelly had quickly latched onto Eliana, and had become a dear friend. In fact, she was going to be Kelly's matron of honor when she married Scott next summer. Besides Kelly, many of the women at church had become close friends, and their house seemed to be continually filled with high school students.

"How about you Evan? How is married life?"

"It's been everything I had hoped it would be. Eliana is a wonderful partner, and friend, and I'm looking forward to what the future holds."

"Now we have to talk about your shocking proposal. It absolutely stunned the nation. Social media exploded with reactions – some favorable and some not so favorable. Did you have any doubts when you made that decision?" Martha schooled her feature into interest, although Eliana was certain she was more concerned about how she looked on camera than what Evan had to say.

"I did have doubts," he admitted. "I had no doubts about wanting to be with Eliana, but I had lots of doubts about how it would be received, how it would affect her, what the other women would think and feel about it, and those were things that took some serious consideration. I prayed about it, and talked with my 'fave four'," he smiled as he mentioned the group of women who had helped him make his decision. "We decided that it was the only way to do it properly and that most people would understand, and the ones that didn't," he shrugged, "well, that's their loss."

"Were you really surprised?" Martha turned with a fake smile. "Didn't you see it coming at all?"

"I really was. We both knew that we had feelings for each other, but I was so convinced that the only way to end the show was with him picking one of the twelve women that I didn't see it coming at all."

"Speaking of the twelve women, let's see how the past year has treated them," Martha smiled into the camera.

Evan put his arm around Eliana, and she leaned into him as they watched on the monitor the series of updates. Many of them had kept in touch with them, and they really felt like they had friends for life.

Sarah Partridge was written in a fancy script on the screen before the bubbly blonde appeared walking in her family's orchard. There seemed to be a new sense of maturity to her, and her eyes didn't seem to sparkle as much as they had a year ago.

"It wasn't long after I returned from Los Angeles that my father had a stroke. Although we prayed for a miracle, he never recovered." A tear trickled down her cheek. "It became more important than ever that I remain here, and I realized that there was a reason Evan and I couldn't be together." A young man in jeans and a warm coat entered and wrapped his arm around Sarah. "Michael has been helping at the orchard for many years, but only this last summer did he let me know that he had been interested in me for a long time."

Michael looked at the camera and confessed, "I was hoping that Evan wouldn't pick her throughout the show, but I couldn't see how he wouldn't fall in love with her. I think I actually cheered when she left the ballroom." A flashback to that moment from the show was played. "I knew she was hurting, but it also made me aware that I needed to let her know how I felt, or I could lose her for good."

"I loved my time on *The Twelve Dates of Christmas*, but I'm glad to be home."

One by one the girls had their moment to catch their fans up on their lives. Paloma Valdez had a reptile enclosure named after her at the zoo. She had been on several dates since the program, but hadn't found anyone who really fit with her.

Lisette Blanchard told about how her family had seen her on the program and when they realized how much she missed them, they came to see her. Two of her sisters now worked in Le Poulet Rouge with her.

Robyn Talbot was still dominating the mobile phone world in southern California, and hinted that there might be a man in her life although she didn't name anyone specific. Evan and Eliana knew that it was the saxophonist from the jazz band that Evan had taken her to see.

Yi Wang's jewelry had seen a surge in popularity since being featured on the show. The pieces created with the gems that Evan had given her had not only been beautiful, but had sold for quite a large sum as well. She had designed both Evan's and Eliana's wedding bands as a thank you for allowing her to be part of the show and a sign of their friendship that she hoped would be as enduring as their marriage.

Jillian Gosling had met a guy online who had been rooting for her during the show. He worked at a different wildlife preserve and also had a love of geese in particular.

Kirstin Schwann had moved from Arizona to southern California to be near her snorkeling instructor boyfriend. She still coached a high school swim team, but now spent all her off time on the beach. There was no mention that their relationship had begun on the show although viewers were likely to recognize him from that episode.

Marian Merkel's cheese had seen the same popularity explosion that Yi's jewelry had. She had needed to hire some help to keep up with demands. She still enjoyed movies, and had hinted not so subtly to Eliana that if she had an extra spot at any Hollywood premieres or galas that she would be happy to attend. Eliana already planned to have a special invitation sent to her for the premiere of her next movie.

Clara Parker was still dancing in starring roles in New York, but she also took time to visit local ballet studios, particularly those in poverty stricken areas to encourage young ladies to follow their dreams. She had also started a foundation named after her mom to provide dance scholarships for low income families.

Emma Laird was still at Iowa State University and had started dating one of the trainers in the athletic department. She had come to visit Eliana and Evan on a few occasions, and they had been pleased to find that she had come to terms with not being chosen, and now was a close friend.

Kaydence Ochoa had continued her push for her second childhood. While she still kept her position in the symphony, on her off times she went to art classes, amusement parks, zoos, parks, and anywhere else she thought might be fun. A few of her friends had joined her and they had started a blog called "Kids Again" detailing their adventures.

Finally, Harmony Lancaster's band, Pink Aftermath, had been discovered when they had been shown on the program. They now had an album released with one of the songs in particular doing impressively well, and currently she was on tour.

Evan and Eliana were both pleased to see that all of the women were doing well, and that the show had seemed to impact all of them positively in one respect or another. As the updates finished, Martha turned her attention back to them.

"The elopement – tell us why you chose that instead of a more formal wedding." She made it almost sound like an accusation. Not surprising since the media had acted like it was a personal attack on them that they had slipped away to be married not giving them the satisfaction of a large, over the top wedding.

"It was a sudden decision really," Eliana explained as she looked into her husband's eyes. "I was about to go to Australia to film a movie, and we decided we didn't want to wait any more."

Evan smiled lovingly at her. "We went to our small church in Merryton with my family and hers, and were married there."

A photo was shown behind them with Eliana in a simple white dress with a full skirt that skimmed her knees and Evan in a suit looking at each other adoringly in front of the small white chapel. Eliana clutched a small bunch of daisies in one hand.

"How did your family feel about the suddenness of the wedding?" Martha asked Eliana.

"They were ecstatic. They were afraid that it would be a large event that they couldn't afford or that would make them feel insignificant with the crush of people around. So a simple wedding was a relief for them in a lot of ways."

Another photo appeared on the screen with both sides of the family clustered around Eliana and Evan.

"And they were just happy that you finally married me," Evan teased.

Eliana nudged him, but smiled. "They fell in love with you at Thanksgiving before the show even happened."

"That's something that's worth noting," Martha jumped in. "Although it seemed sudden to the rest of the nation, your relationship had begun before the show even started in a lot of ways. In fact, many of the women on the show thought that Evan's heart might already belong to someone else. Did any of them suspect it was Eliana?"

"There were a few who I think suspected Eliana in particular, and many others who thought it might be one of the other ladies although they didn't know exactly who it might be," Evan admitted. "Kaydence was the one who openly asked me if I was in love with Eliana, and I admitted to her I was when she promised to keep it a secret. Later when I was consulting with my 'fave four' she said that although she hadn't told them, the rest had figured it out as well."

"Was it difficult for you to watch Evan date these other women?" Martha directed the question to Eliana.

"Absolutely, but I had made a promise from the very beginning that I would show all of the women at their very best, and make America want to cheer for each of them. Keeping that in mind helped me to view their dates more professionally and less personally."

Martha turned to Evan. "I imagine it was less difficult to date all these lovely women than it was for Eliana to have to watch it." She gave a knowing grin that made Eliana want to slap her.

“I think in some ways it was more difficult, because she was able to distance herself from the situation to some extent while I was in the middle of it all. And in the end it had to be my decision. I’ve already told you what a struggle that was.”

“Do you regret being on the show?” Martha asked.

Evan looked at Eliana. “Not for a moment. It wasn’t easy, but I wouldn’t have known Eliana without the show.” He smiled impishly. “My true love gave me twelve dates for Christmas, and they only made me love her even more.”

“How sweet,” Martha said insincerely. “So what’s next for ‘Eviana’?” She grinned as she used the media’s favorite pet name for the couple.

“Eliana recently finished directing an action movie which will be released this summer,” Evan said proudly. “It’s going to be great. I had the privilege of watching a lot of the filming, and it was amazing.”

“It was definitely a dream come true for me,” Eliana admitted. “I’ve wanted to do an action movie for a long time so I jumped at the opportunity. But I may be pulling back on my directing for a little while,” she smiled at Evan.

“We can announce it now, I was offered the defensive coordinator position at Central Michigan, and we’ll be moving there after the school year is over. I’ll miss my team at Merryton High, but I’ve told them that I’m going to keep my eye on them.” He held Eliana’s hand. “Eliana has decided that with the craziness of training, games, and recruiting, that it would be easier for her to stay more local for directing positions."

"I don't want to be away from him any more than I have to," Eliana admitted to Martha, "especially now that we have a baby on the way."

The shocked look on Martha's face was priceless, but it quickly turned to glee when she realized that she was the one who would get credit for 'breaking the story' even though she had nothing to do with it. "Congratulations to both of you! That is exciting news indeed!" She faced the camera. "A year after *The Twelve Dates of Christmas* and so much has happened for each of the people involved. I hope you've enjoyed seeing how your favorites are doing. I'd like to thank the twelve ladies, as well as Evan Garnett and Eliana Santos . . ."

"Garnett," Eliana interrupted.

"Excuse me," Martha barely refrained from scowling at her.

"It's Eliana Garnett now." Eliana wiggled her fingers with her wedding ring on it as a reminder of her new status.

Martha forced a smile. "Of course. As well as Evan and Eliana *Garnett* for being part of our program. Have a Merry Christmas." As soon as the all clear was given, Martha shot out of her chair and bolted from the room muttering the whole way and followed by her harried assistants.

Evan chuckled. "Someone's not very merry this year."

Eliana snuggled into him. "She's just jealous that she doesn't have someone like you."

"Somehow I don't think that's it," Evan replied although he tightened his arm around her and kissed her head.

"Did you mean that part at the end about the dates making you love me more?"

Tilting her head to face him, Evan answered, "Every one of those dates only reminded me of how much I would rather be with you, and every moment I'm with you makes me thank God for the wisdom he gave at the finale so that we could be together." He lowered his mouth to hers, and there were no more doubts. Eliana knew that though there were twelve incredible women he could have chosen, it was her he loved, and he always would.

Made in the USA
Columbia, SC
27 July 2023